THE M

Slocum galloped after the rider, only to slow when the man twisted about and discharged the shotgun. The pellets went wide, missing Slocum by a country mile. If he rode closer, though, he stood the chance of catching enough lead to hurt. Drawing his six-shooter, Slocum leveled it and fired once. At this range, he had little hope of hitting the rider. And he didn't. All he succeeded in doing was adding some speed to the man's departure.

Following at a greater distance, Slocum wanted to find out what was going on. But a turn in the road gave the man he pursued the chance to disappear. The road straightened and worked uphill, giving Slocum a good view for almost a quarter mile. The empty road mocked him. He looked around for any hint that he had ridden into an ambush . . .

JAKE LOGAN

SLOCUM'S FOUR BRIDES

J

JOVE BOOKS, NEW YORK

THE BERKLEY PUBLISHING GROUP
Published by the Penguin Group
Penguin Group (USA) Inc.
375 Hudson Street, New York, New York 10014, USA
Penguin Group (Canada), 90 Eglinton Avenue East, Suite 700, Toronto, Ontario M4P 2Y3, Canada
(a division of Pearson Penguin Canada Inc.)
Penguin Books Ltd., 80 Strand, London WC2R 0RL, England
Penguin Group Ireland, 25 St. Stephen's Green, Dublin 2, Ireland (a division of Penguin Books Ltd.)
Penguin Group (Australia), 250 Camberwell Road, Camberwell, Victoria 3124, Australia
(a division of Pearson Australia Group Pty. Ltd.)
Penguin Books India Pvt. Ltd., 11 Community Centre, Panchsheel Park, New Delhi—110 017, India
Penguin Group (NZ), 67 Apollo Drive, Rosedale, North Shore 0632, New Zealand
(a division of Pearson New Zealand Ltd.)
Penguin Books (South Africa) (Pty.) Ltd., 24 Sturdee Avenue, Rosebank, Johannesburg 2196,
South Africa

Penguin Books Ltd., Registered Offices: 80 Strand, London WC2R 0RL, England

This is a work of fiction. Names, characters, places, and incidents either are the product of the author's imagination or are used fictitiously, and any resemblance to actual persons, living or dead, business establishments, events, or locales is entirely coincidental.

SLOCUM'S FOUR BRIDES

An Jove Book / published by arrangement with the author

PRINTING HISTORY
Jove edition / January 2008

Copyright © 2008 by The Berkley Publishing Group.
Cover illustration by Sergio Giovine.

ISBN: 978-0-515-14396-6

JOVE®
Jove Books are published by The Berkley Publishing Group,
a division of Penguin Group (USA) Inc.,
375 Hudson Street, New York, New York 10014.
JOVE is a registered trademark of Penguin Group (USA) Inc.
The "J" design is a trademark belonging to Penguin Group (USA) Inc.

PRINTED IN THE UNITED STATES OF AMERICA

10 9 8 7 6 5 4 3 2 1

1

The fist swinging straight for John Slocum's face was the size of a Virginia ham. Slocum ducked and barely got out of the way of the blow, which would have left his face a bloody pulp.

"Come on and fight, you lily-livered pup," the man facing Slocum roared. From the way the mountain of a man squared his shoulders and held his huge fists, Slocum knew he faced a pugilist. He had no chance to take down a man used to fighting bare-knuckle for a hundred rounds.

"You got it all wrong," Slocum said, circling. If he kept moving, he might figure out a way to avoid getting his head knocked off. The fighter advanced faster than Slocum would have thought a man that size could and landed a hard punch in the center of Slocum's chest. He staggered back, unable to breathe.

"Come on, fight. You welshed on the debt. You gonna show ever'one how big a coward you are?"

Slocum wished he still wore his cross-draw holster with the Colt Navy slung in it. It would get the law on his trail, shooting an unarmed man, but Slocum felt like the one who was unarmed in this fight. He looked around. His breathing was labored from the punch. He saw no one willing to take his case. If anything, the men in the circle were all too intent on betting against him.

"I'll pay off Jenks," Slocum gasped out. He staggered and almost fell. Every breath sucked liquid fire into his lungs. He shook his head to clear it in time to see the man rushing him. Getting caught up in a bear hug was as likely to mean his death as being beaten to a bloody pulp.

Slocum barely avoided the bull's rush. He felt fingers clutching at his arm to hold him, but he jerked free and stumbled back into the middle of the barroom floor.

"You're a damn liar as well as a thief," the man said. He sneered. Slocum saw the man had lost two front teeth in some prior fight. For the life of him, he could not imagine what the man had fought to end up damaged like that. Maybe a grizzly bear? "He sold you to me. I ain't had any fun lately, Slocum, so I get to bust you up good."

He lumbered forward, fists swinging. Slocum backed up, only to run into the ring of men surrounding him. They pushed him forward so hard that he stumbled. As he was falling, he realized they had saved him from another of those sledgehammer blows. The fighter gave a mighty swing, which missed again. Slocum landed on his knees and then scrambled to get around and into the center of the ring, where he could dodge and duck.

He settled down, the initial surprise at such a vicious opponent passing. He coldly watched for an opening. When he saw it, he swung. His fist struck the man's belly, and Slocum thought he had hit a brick wall. He danced away, twisted, and kicked hard. His boot landed on the man's kneecap, staggering him.

The grunt of pain was all he got in the way of reward, though. Slocum began systematically punching, finding vulnerable spots and landing his blows so hard that his knuckles turned raw. Worse than the pain he was getting in his hands, he wasn't delivering much damage to the man.

Slocum knew that a single punch from either of those mule-kick-strong fists would kill him.

"I'll pay back the money. I got some coming," Slocum said. He knew it wouldn't matter. Jenks had sent this mountain of a man to kill him. The roar of the crowd faded away as Slocum concentrated.

He had come to Salt Lake City thinking to find some work, but jobs had been scarce. The railroad had already passed through, and construction was at an end. No mining. What ranching went on was done on such a small scale that most of the huge Mormon families supplied more than enough hands to run their own herds. He was so down he would have even considered sheepherding for a spell, but there was none of that to be had, either.

Helping a friend had gotten him into this mess. Lemuel Sanders had needed a stake for prospecting, and Slocum had given him what he had and then some. He should never have borrowed the fifty dollars from Jenks. The man had presented himself as a legitimate businessman willing to take a risk and had agreed Slocum had six months to pay back the money. Lemuel had insisted he would find a sure-fire claim over in Colorado in less time. Lemuel had not been gone quite that long, and Jenks wanted his money back.

Slocum had no real expectation of Lemuel striking it rich in such a short time, but they had met a couple years back, and Slocum had been impressed by how astute a prospector his new friend was. Wild and often drunk, reckless to the point of getting tossed into the calaboose in about every town he passed through, Lemuel knew how to find blue dirt laden with gold.

Slocum had figured he would get the money back to Jenks and then move on, but the money had been hard to find.

"I've still got a week," Slocum said, circling his opponent and forcing the bigger man to use up his energy. This tactic usually worked. The huge man was like a storm whipping across the plains, though; his energy built rather than diminished.

"You got no time," the man cried. He rushed Slocum and landed another stunning blow to Slocum's chest. For an instant Slocum thought his heart would explode, and the world turned watery around him. His legs sagged, and he fought to keep from blacking out. A weak punch in reply got lucky. He broke the man's nose and sent blood flying out in a shower that got the crowd excited again. The betting intensified, and Slocum reckoned some of the money was now on him to win—or maybe to not die as quick.

Slocum could not continue much longer. He staggered back and watched as his nemesis came after him again. Slocum stamped down hard on the boards under his feet, sending the loose end in front of his opponent sailing into the air. It caught the man just below the knee and broke his stride, and tumbling off balance, the man stepped into the hole left by the raised board. He fell through the gap to his knee.

Slocum moved like lightning. Before the man could get out of the hollow in the floor, Slocum launched a kick that landed behind the man's other knee. This brought him face-down. Slocum began stomping on him, boots aimed at the man's face and head. One or two of the vicious kicks found their target. This took some of the fight out of the giant of a man. Some. Slocum kept kicking. His arms hung like leaden weights, and any punch he might deliver wouldn't harm a lamb. By the time he was panting with exertion, he had done enough damage to lay the man out flat.

"Finish him off," someone called. "Olaf's a son of a bitch. He done kilt more men than any of us kin remember. You do him good, mister. Kill him!"

"Where's my six-gun?" Slocum took the gun and belt in shaking hands and pulled out the Colt Navy. He cocked it, and the crowd turned quiet in expectation. Spinning in a circle, Slocum pointed the gun in turn at everyone around him. "There's not going to be anybody killed. Unless it's one of you."

"Aw, mister, go on. We got money bet that somebody'd die. We lose our bet if—" The man clamped his mouth shut when Slocum aimed his .36-caliber pistol at the speaker's face.

"Does it matter *who* dies? It could be you. Get away. All of you."

The ring of spectators grumbled but obeyed. Slocum turned back to the man on the floor—in the floor—moaning as he regained consciousness. *Indestructible* described the man better than anything else Slocum could come up with.

He knelt down and poked the muzzle of his six-shooter into the man's face.

"I can pull the trigger," Slocum said coldly, "but I'm not going to. Unless I have to. I have no quarrel with you. What's it going to be? Blood all over the floor, or a truce?"

"My blood?" The huge man swiped at his still-bleeding nose.

"Your call," Slocum said.

"You're mighty good," the giant said, "fer a little fella."

"Did Jenks come to you or was it the other way around?"

"I don't know you from Adam," the man said. When he tried to pull his leg free from the floorboards, Slocum shoved him back down. Keeping him immobile while they worked things out looked to be the safest course. "Jenks come to me, said he wanted you all busted up. Didn't much care if I kilt you. I ain't kilt nobody in close to a month and was gettin' the urge. You know what I mean?"

Slocum did.

"You'll be dead if I lay eyes on you again," Slocum said. "Stay away from Jenks, too."

"You gonna settle a score with him?"

Slocum did not answer. There was no reason, because the man read the answer on Slocum's face.

As Slocum strapped on his gun belt, he glared at the proprietor of the saloon. Salt Lake City regulations required everyone to leave their firearms at the door. Things were done differently in Mormon country. This saloon was off the main street, almost hidden, because the Mormons frowned on serving alcohol. Try as they might to prohibit it in Salt Lake City, they realized it would cause more trouble than they could handle if they succeeded, so they turned a blind eye to establishments like Rose's Teahouse and Imbibing Emporium.

"Fix the loose board in the floor," Slocum said to the barkeep as he left. He was in sore need of a drink but was not inclined to remain one second longer. He had barely left his six-shooter with the guard at the door when he had been attacked.

Jenks had to answer for that.

Slocum stepped out on a bustling thoroughfare. At the far end of the wide street stood the Mormon Tabernacle, its gold figure of an angel high on its spire. Slocum was in such a mood that he considered finding out if the Angel Moroni was real gold. A few ounces scraped off or a trumpet removed from an angelic hand might repay him for getting the shit beat out of him. Every movement brought fresh agony.

He had only been tapped a couple times but worried that he might have a broken rib. Pressing his fingers into his chest sent new waves of pain through his torso, but the sharp, breathtaking jab that went with a broken rib was missing. He didn't have to pull up his shirt to know he sported some colorful, nasty bruises, though.

He stopped to rest in the shade of a tree and regain some of his strength.

"Mighty impressive fight, mister."

Slocum's hand flashed to the ebony handle of his six-gun, but he did not draw. Standing a couple paces away, hands out at his sides to show he wasn't armed or going for a weapon, was a smallish man with a face like a marmot. His nose even twitched the same as the small rodent's. All that was missing were long white whiskers. The man's hair was about the right shade of brown, and his deep-set eyes were black as lumps of coal.

"Not what I went in there looking for," Slocum said. He left his hand resting on the butt of his six-shooter, though he knew this would draw unwanted attention. The police in this town were ever vigilant about keeping the peace. He moved his hand away. The rodent-man approached.

"I'm looking for a man of your toughness for a job."

"I don't kill people." Slocum laughed ruefully. "Today it's all I can do to keep myself alive."

"That's the very quality in need to hire out," the man said. "My name's Rufus Preen."

Slocum nodded rather than taking the small man's hand proffered for a handshake. "I'm Slocum."

"Slocum, yes," Preen said. "Well, Mr. Slocum, this is my proposition: I need an escort for some valuable property on its way to Colorado. If you would protect it and see that it is all delivered to various purchasers, I will reward you handsomely."

"How handsomely?"

Preen smiled. Slocum wished he would stop. He had two protruding front teeth, making his resemblance to a rat even more extreme.

"Fifty dollars."

For a moment, Slocum started to laugh. This had to be some joke Jenks was playing on him. Then he saw that Preen was serious.

"You know a man named Jenks?"

Preen frowned as he concentrated, then nodded slowly. "The name is familiar. He is a rather disreputable sort who loans money at high interest rates."

"I borrowed fifty dollars from him to outfit a friend damned near six months ago."

"Your friend must be fortunate knowing a man like you. Going into debt with a jackal like Jenks is a serious matter. That you have not hightailed it shows your desire to be an honest borrower and to repay. I like that, too." Preen's face unscrewed and his eyes went wider. "My God, man, was that fight over your debt to Jenks?"

"Seemed that way," Slocum said.

"Jenks will not stop at sending a single man after you. He employs dozens of hired killers." Preen studied Slocum a bit more, then hastily added, "Not that you cannot take care of yourself. That's why I sought your employment." Preen backed off. "I am sorry to have taken your time, Mr. Slocum."

"Because I owe Jenks, you're not willing to hire me?"

"I have no dealings with owlhoots like Jenks. My business is legitimate. Entirely."

"I like the idea of having to take your cargo to Colorado," Slocum said. "That's where my friend went."

"I . . . well, that would seem to be a decent resolution to your problem," Preen said.

"If I paid Jenks the fifty dollars you're willing to give me for this chore, I wouldn't have anything left for supplies. Where in Colorado do I have to deliver your goods? Denver?"

"No, no, not so far. A mining camp on the other side of Douglas Pass. And I would provide a wagon, team, and all provisions. I could hardly have you skimping on provisions."

"I'd have to leave soon," Slocum said. He glanced up at the distant Wasatch Mountains and the storm wreathing the highest peaks. "Winter's on its way. An early snow might close the passes."

"That is why I am, uh, somewhat in need of retaining an employee as quickly as possible."

"In desperate need," Slocum corrected. Try as he might, Preen could not hide the look on his face that confirmed this. "I've been in Salt Lake City for a spell. There are any number of others looking for work. I can't believe I'm the only one you can hire."

"This is a very religious town," Preen said. "What you would be protecting along the route is not very popular with the local townspeople. Quite the contrary, in fact."

Slocum nodded in understanding. It seemed to him much of the commerce in Salt Lake City was conducted as if through a blockade. Black market goods were easily found as the town fathers looked the other way, but if Preen had cargo of sufficient value going into a Colorado mining camp, it might be hard finding anyone in Salt Lake City willing to escort it.

"I want the fifty dollars up front," Slocum said.

Preen hesitated.

"You have my word. I'll see your cargo to wherever you want it delivered, but you have to pay me now."

"Deal!" Preen shoved out his hand again. This time Slocum shook. Preen fumbled in his pocket and found fifty dollars in scrip, handing it to Slocum as if he were giving up an arm and a leg.

Slocum tucked the money into his vest pocket.

"When do I leave?"

"The stable on the eastern side of town—Smith and Sons?"

"I know it," Slocum said. It wasn't too far from where he had stabled his own horse.

"Tomorrow at dawn. I'll have the wagon loaded and ready to roll." Preen licked his thin lips nervously and added, "You *will* be there?"

"I shook on it. You have my word." Sincerity rang in his words like a gold coin dropped on a bar, but Preen was still upset.

"You intend to pay Jenks, don't you?"

Slocum nodded.

"That's what worries me. You might have agreed, but Jenks obviously has other ideas."

"Let me worry about Jenks," Slocum said. "He'll get his due."

Preen glanced at Slocum's holstered six-shooter, then nervously bobbed his head and rushed off.

"Wait!" Slocum called after him, but the mousy man had rounded the corner of a building and was gone. He had wanted to ask what the cargo was. Slocum shrugged it off. He had a bigger problem to deal with right now.

A problem named Jenks.

2

Jenks was a king seated on his throne. The three-story brick building might as well have been a castle with battlements. As Slocum walked past slowly, he saw riflemen posted in the upper windows. Anyone trying to get in the front door without Jenks's permission would be ventilated fast. He kept walking, turned the corner, then went to a store across the street.

"What's that building over there?" Slocum asked the shopkeeper. The older man wiped dirt from his hands onto an already filthy apron as he shook his head.

"Somewhere you don't want to go. That there's Lucas Jenks's place. He fancies himself a banker, but he finances most every illegal thing going on in Salt Lake City."

"Do tell," Slocum said. He picked over the fruit displayed outside the store, found himself an apple without too many worms, and paid a nickel for it. He chomped down on the juicy fruit as he walked back past Jenks's headquarters. By the time he had finished his apple, he had spotted the weakness and how to get inside.

As workmen unloaded a wagon behind the building, Slocum grabbed a heavy gray canvas apron and slung it around his waist to hide his six-shooter. He hoisted a crate to

11

his shoulder and staggered under the weight. Not only was the box heavier than he expected, his ribs were paining him from the beating he had received. Slocum sucked in a breath and held it, since doing anything else was too painful. He maneuvered himself around stacked boxes and into the storeroom of Jenks's headquarters, dropped the crate on a pile, then lit out when he saw stairs leading upward.

"Hey, where the hell you goin'?" called the foreman of the workmen unloading the wagon.

"Be right back," Slocum said. "He sent word he wanted to see me."

"You poor son of a bitch," the foreman said, shaking his head. He returned to his chores, thinking Slocum was in for trouble, when it was the other way around. Jenks had no idea how big a bite he had chewed off sending the giant of a mountain man to whomp up on Slocum.

A man slept in a chair, rocked back so only the two back legs of the chair were on the floor. His hat was pulled down over his eyes to shade his face from the sunlight slanting through the south window. Slocum considered what it meant having an armed, if sleepy, man here to block his retreat. Then he walked softly past, opened the door, and peered inside.

Jenks sat at a table laden with food, forking in one mouthful after another. He faced another door on the far side of the room. Slocum closed the door softly behind him, reached under his apron, and drew his six-gun.

The distinctive metallic click as he cocked it caused Jenks to freeze.

"Who's there? That you, Roy?"

"Roy's got other concerns right about now," Slocum said, guessing the name of the sleeping guard. "You might say he's enjoying sweet dreams."

"He'll be taking a dirt nap when I get my hands on him. He—"

"Shut up," Slocum said coldly. He laid his six-gun's

barrel against the side of Jenks's head. "You sent a man to kill me. I don't like that."

"You was behind on payment."

"We're even now," Slocum said, dropping the green-backs on the man's plate. Gravy began soaking into the paper money. Jenks tentatively stuck his fork into it and held up a note.

"You're out of your mind, Slocum," he said. "What do you think? That this will make us square?"

"I borrowed fifty. That's fifty. We're even."

"I charge interest. I—"

"Whatever you paid that dumb galoot I beat up over at Rose's is your loss. Count it as interest you received from me but misspent."

"That don't make a lick of sense."

"Then think on this: If you try to kill me again, it'll be you out there north of town pushing up daisies in the potter's field," Slocum said. "You don't have enough men in this building or in the entire damn town to stop me before I put a slug into your heart."

"Nobody's that good a shot."

"I'm an exception," Slocum said, not bothering to appreciate Jenks's small joke. "You understand? We're even. You have your money."

"That's what you say. If you could get fifty, you can get me the rest. Another fifty."

"You are either the dumbest man I've ever seen or the greediest. Either way, you'll be the deadest before I pay you one more red cent." Slocum moved the muzzle around and thrust it into Jenks's ear until he saw sweat beginning to bead on the man's forehead. For all his braggadocio, Jenks was scared shitless.

Slocum stepped back, then quickly swung his Colt, laying the barrel alongside Jenks's skull. The dull *thunk* told Slocum he had hit Jenks with just the right force. The man collapsed into his plate, moaning. Not wasting any time,

Slocum retreated and got through the door and past the sleeping Roy to find the stairs. The foreman had stacked the last of the crates. He looked up in surprise.

"Didn't reckon to ever see you again." The man frowned. "Who the hell are you? I don't remember hirin' you."

"I quit," Slocum said, tossing him the canvas apron. He slipped through the door as he heard a commotion upstairs. He stepped out into the bright afternoon sunlight of Salt Lake City, feeling better than he had in ages. All his debts were paid, and all he had to do was drive a supply wagon into Colorado, where he intended going anyhow. It was about time he collected the money he had loaned Lemuel Sanders.

Just before dawn, Slocum rode slowly to the Smith and Sons Livery. He kept a sharp eye out for anyone Jenks might have sent to put a bullet in his head. How likely that was depended on how many of Jenks's men had seen their boss humiliated. Slocum hoped that Jenks kept the matter to himself and spent the fifty dollars well. That wasn't likely to happen, but Slocum was a man of infinite optimism. At times. Mostly he was pragmatic about life and everything it held.

In spite of having seen about everything, though, Slocum could still be surprised. He drew rein beside Preen's wagon and saw the cargo, not yet covered with a tarpaulin. Four large chests were already secured there, one with its lid open. It was filled with women's clothing.

"This your cargo?" Slocum asked the rodentlike man. Rufus Preen's eyes darted about as if he had been cornered, then he looked up at Slocum. A tiny smile danced on his lips.

"It's all legit. Every bit of it."

"I didn't know there was a lot of smuggling going on in women's clothes," Slocum said. He dismounted and checked the rest of the cargo. There was a considerable amount of food for the trail. More than five people could eat. He reckoned most of it was destined for sale to miners hungry for something other than beans and salt pork. But there was a considerable amount of space in the wagon bed where nothing had been stowed. "What's going in there?"

"I am, unless I get to sit with you."

Slocum turned and saw a short blonde woman with the bluest eyes this side of heaven. She had a button nose and cute dimples. Most of her hair had been tucked away under a sunbonnet, and she wore a sturdy gingham dress that barely came down to the tops of her shoes. Slocum found himself wondering about those ankles, the legs, and what else lay hidden by the thick clothing. Her blouse was well filled, and she took note of how he looked at her by thrusting out her chest just a bit more. She stood with her hip cocked to one side and her balled-up hand resting on it.

"You must be a passenger," Slocum said, glancing in Preen's direction. The man had said nothing about passengers, but the blonde woman explained the chest filled with women's clothing.

"That I am. Sarah June Barlow."

"Miss Barlow." Slocum tipped his hat to her. "Get on in and we'll be off right away."

"In a hurry, sir?" Sarah June asked, amused at something Slocum could not figure.

Slocum wanted to put as much distance between him and Salt Lake City as he could. There had not been any trace of trouble brewing because of his run-in with Jenks, but he felt more comfortable out on the trail. Even the buzzards and coyotes were better companions than Jenks.

Having Sarah June Barlow as a traveling companion was a bonus, considering he had already given up all the money he had been paid for the trip.

"Reckon I'm always antsy to be on the trail, ma'am," Slocum said.

"Call me Sarah June. Please. And may I call you John?"

Slocum looked at her, then at Preen, who shrugged.

"I had to tell them who was driving them to Colorado," Preen said.

"Them?"

Two more women came from inside the livery, fussing and fretting over their trail clothes. One was a strawberry blonde, almost as tall as Slocum and as thin as a rail. The other was a well-endowed brunette who moved with a sashay that made it appear as if her feet didn't touch the earth. There was a haughtiness about her that put Slocum on guard.

"That's Wilhelmina and Betty," said Sarah June. "Our traveling companions."

"Three of them? I want a word with you, Preen."

"Uh, Slocum, you won't be herding three women out there, not at all," said Preen, nibbling at his lower lip and looking upset at the way Slocum glared.

"Good," Slocum said, relief flooding him.

"Mr. Preen's right," Sarah June said brightly. "Tabitha isn't here yet. There're four of us."

"Four?"

"They must be delivered quickly, Slocum," Preen said. "I've already taken the money for them and—"

"Money?" Slocum pinned Preen against the wagon and glared at him. "I don't traffic in human flesh." Although a Southern landholder before the war, he and his family had never kept slaves. His fight had been for Georgia and its right to govern itself without meddling from some far distant Yankee capital. The notion that Preen had gulled him into transporting women sold to a brothel or for some other illicit use rankled. He might have taken Preen's money, but he would not do anything to earn it. How he would return the blood money was something he would worry about later. After he walked away.

"It's not like that, Slocum," Preen blurted. "Not at all."

"He's right, John," spoke up Sarah June. The saucy blonde

moved to stand beside Preen. She even took his hand and held it in her own. This made Preen uncomfortable.

"So what is it, if you're not being sold?" Slocum demanded.

"We've wives, pure and simple," said the brunette, Betty. "That's all we want to be. Just wives."

"*Only* wives," corrected the tall blonde. Wilhelmina spoke with a slight accent Slocum could not place. "We do not stay in this place where they have many wives. We want to be *only* wives."

"You're not Mormons?" Slocum knew a condition of statehood was for the Mormons to give up polygamy, but outside Salt Lake City it was widely practiced. For all he knew, it was a matter of record inside the city, too. Some of the more vocal factions in the church had prevented the statehood vote on account of this one practice, refusing to give up their harems in exchange for the dubious admission to the Union. Slocum doubted Utah would be admitted any time soon because of the furor.

"We are," Sarah June said. "We do not want to share our husbands, though. I was the fifth wife." The bitterness with which she spoke told Slocum there was more to it than she was revealing.

"We all have this problem," Betty said. "One husband and no other wives will be fine. That is why we arranged with Mr. Preen to become mail-order brides."

"There's Tabitha now. Tabitha Smith," Preen said, pointing to distract Slocum.

Slocum glanced over his shoulder and saw a determined woman walking toward them. She made each step as if it took her a foot higher on an impossibly tall mountain, one she would climb come hell or high water.

"Is he our driver?" Tabitha frowned at Slocum. "You have all our belongings in the wagon? Good, let's go."

"Hold your horses," Slocum said. "I'm still conducting business with Preen."

"Do not be impudent, sir," Tabitha said. Her thin lips drew back like a wolf baring its fangs. There was a certain similarity between a hungry wolf and the woman, Slocum decided. Streaks of gray ran through her dark hair, although he doubted she could be thirty years old. Her dark eyes fixed on him and again he got the sensation of being prey rather than someone responsible for getting her safely to her betrothed, whoever that might be.

"How good are you at handling a yoke of oxen?" Slocum asked. Tabitha opened her mouth and then clamped it shut as she considered her arrogant comeback and decided against uttering it.

"I am not experienced that way," she said.

"You might have to be, if you piss me off any more than I already am," Slocum said. He turned back to Preen. The man was trying to slip away. Slocum leaned into Preen, pinning him to the wagon. "Tell me about what I signed up for. All of it."

"I, well, it's as Miss Sarah June said. They are all hunting for a better life."

"With only one husband."

"We had one husband. We didn't like having a dozen co-wives," Tabitha said.

"A dozen?" Sarah June sniffed contemptuously. "I was fifth in line and my husband had already added nine more."

"Then you were lucky. He never saw you and you could do as you chose," said Wilhelmina. "I had to—"

"Ladies, please," Slocum said. "There'll be plenty of time to tell your tales. Right now, I want it straight from Preen." He turned back to the squirming man and let his cold green eyes bore into the man's soul.

"They all want out of town, Slocum," Preen said. "I got them husbands over in Colorado. Miners, mostly. You know how it is. There're a hundred men for every woman. That makes these fine ladies . . ."

"Commodities," Slocum said. "You're peddling humans like they were prize cattle."

"Cattle have no say-so," Tabitha piped up. "We hired Mr. Preen. He hired you. We're going willingly."

"You said you were all married," Slocum said. "That means you all have husbands already." He saw how they exchanged guilty looks. He was right that they were running away from bad marriages—from being part of a harem.

"Our marriages are illegal under the law of the United States," Betty said. "Utah is a territory of the United States, so that means polygamy ought to be illegal. We were forced into our marriages against our wills."

"That makes our marriages shams," Sarah June went on, picking up the argument where Betty stopped. "We were never legally married, so that means we were never married, right?"

"I was married in the tabernacle," Wilhelmina said. "From Sweden I came and I was only a third wife. Thomas preferred his second wife to all his others." Tears welled in the willowy blonde's eyes, but the set to her chin showed how determined she was to leave Salt Lake City and her multiple-wife marriage.

"They have a valid point, Slocum," Preen said. "If they were forced into marriage and their husbands already had wives, that means their husbands were bigamists and were breaking the law."

"Polygamists," Tabitha said. "Not bigamists."

"Yes, yes," Preen rushed on. "You can see that all is legal. They want a single husband, a man to marry under the laws of Colorado. Colorado *is* in the United States of America. Their betrotheds won't be allowed to take more than one spouse."

"Us," Wilhelmina said, wiping away her tears.

"You're not being forced into this?" Slocum asked. He looked from one woman to the next and saw the iron determination in them. He doubted anyone could ever force Tabitha to do anything against her will and wondered how she had ever agreed to a plural marriage, religion or not. In her case, he suspected that having her run away would be a boon to her husband. It might promote more harmony among the remaining wives.

"They won't even notice we're gone," Sarah June assured him. "We mean nothing to them. We want husbands who want only us. Individually."

Slocum could understand that with Sarah June. She was by far the prettiest of the four. But the others were far from ugly, even thin Wilhelmina and the snippy Tabitha. Betty had the appearance of a rich man's wife doing something that was distasteful, but which she was determined to do no matter how much argument she received.

"They're all going of their free wills, Slocum," Preen said. "They're going to a better life."

"In a mining town?" Slocum snorted in disbelief.

"There's more to life than one's surroundings, sir," Tabitha said. "Having a man who dotes on only you is more important than material goods."

"And who knows?" piped up Sarah June. "Our new husbands might strike it rich."

All four of the women nodded at this. Slocum knew they were fooling themselves on that score. Most miners led dirty, dangerous lives and never saw more glitter in their dirt than what it took to eke out a subsistence living. But that did not take away from the women's basic reason for leaving Utah.

"Let's roll," Slocum said. He shot a cold look at Preen, then fastened his horse's reins to the rear of the wagon. Swinging into the driver's seat, he was not surprised to find Sarah June already there. The other three made nests for themselves in the rear of the wagon, spreading blankets to sit on.

"It gets dusty up here, ma'am," Slocum said.

"I am sure it does, John," she answered, "and I thought

I asked you to call me Sarah June. I hardly feel old enough to be called ma'am."

"You're a married woman," Slocum said.

"Not yet." Sarah June turned from him and stared straight ahead. The ice in her voice told Slocum he had touched that sore spot again. He might have gotten the same reaction from any of the women. Shrugging it off, he took the reins and snapped them to get the oxen pulling. He would have preferred mules, but the powerful oxen were still a good choice for dragging the heavily laden wagon up the steep mountain slopes and through Baxter Pass.

"Send a telegram when you ladies get married to your betrotheds," Preen shouted after them. Slocum noted that not one of the women bothered to even wave good-bye to him.

Slocum fell into the rhythm of the wagon rolling up and down on the rocky road as he headed eastward. By midday the women were more relaxed and were chattering among themselves. Slocum was excluded from their gossip but hardly noticed. Driving was a chore requiring constant attention to the road and the oxen.

Somewhere around noon he began to worry that someone was on their trail.

"Time to eat," Slocum said, pulling the wagon over to a copse of aspens.

"Is there time for a proper meal?" Tabitha asked. "I am starved."

Slocum hesitated, then said, "Take your time. I need to scout some."

He dropped to the ground, looked up, and saw Sarah June waiting for him to help her. His hands went around her slender waist. He lifted and she was light as a feather. He deposited her on the ground. She looked up at him with her bright blue eyes, and a smile danced on her lips.

"Want help scouting?" she asked.

This startled him; his mind was already a mile back down the trail.

"Reckon I can do my job."

"But it might be more enjoyable with someone helping," Sarah June said, her meaning quite clear. He wondered if being fifth wife made her horny or if this was just her nature.

"Fix me something special for lunch," he said.

"Oh, I will, John," she said. Her hand brushed across his as she turned. Slocum felt the electric touch and wondered at any man who would pass up such a woman. Or decide to keep a baker's dozen of others.

He mounted his horse and turned back to the road. The four women bustled about, each doing just the right thing to keep out of the others' way. He suspected this was a skill learned by sharing cooking chores with a legion of other women.

"Will you be long, Mr. Slocum?" Betty called.

"Not more than a half hour," he said. He rode to the spot where he had driven off the road and considered hiding the wagon tracks, then decided it was useless. There were no branching roads on the way to the pass through the Rockies. Whoever trailed them knew where they were.

He started back in the direction they had just traveled when Betty called out, "Mr. Slocum, you're scouting in the wrong direction. We're headed that a'way." She pointed toward the mountains ahead.

"Just making sure, ma'am," Slocum said. He trotted off before she had time to ask what it was he was checking. As soon as he was out of sight of the wagon, he cut off the road and threaded his way through juniper and pine, keeping hidden from anyone on their trail.

He had gone only a mile when he spotted the man. Whoever he might be, he was no casual traveler heading in the same direction by accident. He carried a shotgun in the crook of his left arm and was intent on the road, hunting for assurance that the wagon had indeed rolled this way.

Slocum waited for him to pass, then got behind him to find out what the man's business might be.

3

The man must have had eyes in the back of his head, because the instant Slocum swung around, the man ducked low in the saddle and put his spurs to his horse. The animal let out a loud snort and shot forward.

"Hey, wait!" Slocum called. He had wondered about the rider; now he was worried. Whatever brought the man out onto the trail had to mean woe for Slocum.

Slocum galloped after the rider, only to slow when the man twisted about and discharged the shotgun. The pellets went wide, missing Slocum by a country mile. If he rode closer, though, he stood the chance of catching enough lead to hurt. Drawing his six-shooter, Slocum leveled it and fired once. At this range, he had little hope of hitting the rider. And he didn't. All he succeeded in doing was adding some speed to the man's departure.

Following at a greater distance, Slocum wanted to find out what was going on. But a turn in the road gave the man he pursued the chance to disappear. The road straightened and worked uphill, giving Slocum a good view for almost a quarter mile. The empty road mocked him. He looked around for any hint that he had ridden into an ambush.

Not seeing the rider, Slocum dismounted and looked at

the road. He found the twin ruts cut by his wagon and the distinctive oxen hoofprints. His own passage back on horseback further complicated the tracks, but one set from a shod horse ran off the road. It took Slocum only a few seconds to sight along the trail and see that the mysterious rider had made a beeline for a stand of juniper trees.

He could call to the man and maybe draw fire again. Or he could ignore him. Slocum knew that there was a slim chance that the man was simply traveling in the same direction. There was only one trail into Colorado unless a man wanted to pioneer a new route. To get to the other side of the mountains, though, required going through Baxter Pass.

That made the pass into a funnel for anyone on the western side of the mountains. If Slocum didn't deal with the man now, he would have to later.

Approaching the trees on foot, six-gun in hand, Slocum listened hard for any warning. He slipped through the trees and into the heavy undergrowth and finally came to a meadow. The tracks showed that the rider had kept moving and had probably circled to get back onto the road farther east. Slocum slammed his six-shooter into his holster, mounted, and rode back to the road. He trotted along, heading back to where he had left the four women. A smile came to his lips. His luck had certainly changed for the better. Getting free of Jenks on his own terms had been a chore, but escorting the four lovely ladies to their future husbands in Colorado was unexpected lagniappe. Slocum wasn't sure about all four of them being married and at the same time not married, but the way Sarah June eyed him made it easy to forget such legal niceties. It got mighty lonely out on the trail.

Hell, for all that, Slocum had found Salt Lake City to be a mighty lonely place. The Mormons might marry and have a dozen wives, but they kept a tight rein on their town. The few saloons were all hidden away, and he was not sure there was a whore in the entire territory.

Slocum had to laugh ruefully at that. The way things were in Utah, why be a whore when it was easy enough to marry into an extended family?

A gunshot echoed back down the trail. Slocum jerked out of his thoughts and cocked his head to one side, listening for other sounds. None came to him.

He put his heels to his horse and galloped uphill back to the wagon and the four women. His horse was lathered, and he was approaching the edge of his own endurance. In comparison to the women, however, he was in good shape.

"What happened?" Slocum hit the ground and ran a few steps toward Wilhelmina. The woman's hair shone in the bright sunlight to the point where it was almost as washed out and white as her face. The pale blonde stared at him, her hand over her mouth. She stuttered and then let go with a string of words that he took to be Swedish. Slocum didn't understand a thing of what she said.

"In the woods, across the road," Betty said, scowling at Wilhelmina and her incoherence. "Gunfire."

"I heard one shot. Were there others?" Slocum tried to remember what the echo had sounded like. The rider had carried a shotgun. He was certain the report had been caused by a handgun.

"Just one shot," Betty said. She looked distraught but was fighting to keep her panic down.

"Where are the others? Sarah June and Tabitha?"

"We were all in the woods looking for fresh food. I heard the shot and ran back."

"What of her?" Slocum jerked his thumb over his shoulder at Wilhelmina, who still muttered in Swedish.

"She came out of the woods a few seconds after I got here."

Slocum looked at the ground. He could not tell what direction Wilhelmina had come from. The tracks were too confused from the women wandering about.

"Do you know where Sarah June and Tabitha went?"

Betty shook her head. He saw that he would not get anything coherent from Wilhelmina. It was as if the women had never heard a gunshot before. Slocum drew his six-shooter and headed across the road since Betty had claimed the shot came from that direction.

Movement ahead caused Slocum to stop and aim. He lowered his six-gun when Sarah June came from the woods, struggling to hold a skirt laden with blackberries.

"What happened?" Slocum demanded.

"I don't know. The shot was close. Is everyone all right?" Sarah June's cheeks were flushed and her eyes bright with fear. She clung to the edge of her skirt, trying to hold in the berries she had collected. She dropped more than she kept as she swayed from side to side, trying to point Slocum in the right direction.

"Get on back to the wagon," Slocum said. "Get under it and don't stick your head out. Was Tabitha with you?"

"I didn't see her."

Slocum brushed past her. For a moment he felt the woman's heat, then he plunged into the forest, leaving Sarah June to fend for herself. The cool dark woods engulfed him and muffled sounds. Slocum slowed, then halted. He turned slowly, straining to hear or see movement. A rabbit flushed from a bramble bush nearby, causing Slocum to almost trigger a shot. He came out of his crouch and worked deeper into the woods.

The snap of a twig breaking alerted Slocum of someone close by. He found a game trail and knelt beside it. When he saw Tabitha on the path, he rose and called to her.

"Oh!" she cried, putting her hand to her breast. "You startled me. What's going on?"

"Betty and Wilhelmina said they heard a gunshot," Slocum said.

"I did, too, but I couldn't tell where it came from."

"What's wrong with your hand?"

"I . . . I burned it. I'm not too good at cooking and accidently touched the coffeepot."

Slocum peered at the woman's burned hand. At least it might have been a burn. Or it could have been caused by not holding tightly enough on to the butt of a six-shooter when she fired it. Checkered grips could tear up an inexperienced gunman's hand.

Gunman—or gun woman.

"Did you hear anything else besides the gunshot?" Slocum's mind raced. The man with the shotgun had been possessed of a guilty conscience to hightail it off the way he had. Or maybe he had a mission that didn't include Slocum. Four women had left their husbands back in Salt Lake City. Devout Mormons might take it poorly and want their wives back badly enough to kill.

Tabitha shook her head.

"Can you find the wagon? Stay with the other women while I scout a bit more," Slocum said. Tabitha stared at him when he made no move to holster his six-shooter.

"Is there anything I can do?"

"Stay out of my line of fire," Slocum said harshly. Tabitha recoiled, as if he had struck her. Without a word, she stepped off the game trail, circled him, and then ran off. He thought she was crying. Slocum had no time to coddle the woman.

Following the game trail a bit farther, Slocum heard a horse softly whinnying. He homed in on it and found the horse tethered to a low-hanging oak tree limb. Not ten feet away he saw a pair of boots poking out from under a blackberry bush. Advancing cautiously, Slocum worked his way around to a spot where he could see the man's face.

He didn't recognize him, but the shotgun beside him looked familiar. Slocum frowned. The report that had echoed down the road hadn't been the bull-throated roar of a shotgun, it had been a pistol. Slocum worked through the thorn bushes, kicked the shotgun away, and only then rolled the man over. A single bullet had caught the man in the middle of his forehead. Slocum had seen men shot this way before. They died fast, usually before they could collapse to the ground.

Slocum searched through the man's pockets and found a small wad of greenbacks. He tucked the six dollar bills into his own pocket. The money wouldn't do the man any good in this world. Under the body, pressed into the dirt, Slocum found a quarter of a silver dollar. It had been sawed jaggedly and a hole drilled through it, as if once strung on a leather strap. The man had nothing in any of his other vest pockets. Slocum pocketed the quarter hunk of dollar. The silver was worth something, even if the coin had been destroyed. Other than the money, there was nothing to identify the man.

Sitting back on his haunches, Slocum studied the man and his clothing. From the cut of his clothing, the man was not likely to be from Salt Lake City. More likely he was a miner, judging by the canvas britches and the heavy cotton shirt. Slocum picked up the shotgun, broke open the action, and looked inside. One shell had been fired. He snorted. He knew who had been on the receiving end of that barrel. The second barrel still carried an unspent shell.

He poked a little around the hole in the man's forehead but could not decide what caliber bullet had made the hole. There was no exit wound, so he had either been shot with a small-caliber round close up or with a heavier bullet from some distance. Slocum hefted the shotgun. No reason to let it rust in the forest. He circled the body, hunting for any trace of the killer.

The ground was so overgrown that he couldn't find anything but a few broken twigs. He plucked blackberries from the bush and ate them as he prowled about, but he soon tired of the chore. There was no point in figuring out who had shot the man since he had no idea who the man even was.

"Somebody saved me the trouble," Slocum finally decided. Then he found himself faced with a dilemma. He heaved a sigh, then trudged back to the wagon, where the four women huddled underneath.

"John, John!" cried Sarah June. She scrambled out and ran to him. "Are you all right?"

"No reason not to be," he said, wondering what had gotten into her. If there had been gunfire, the question might have carried some meaning. He dropped the shotgun into the back of the wagon, then grabbed a small shovel Preen had seen fit to pack. "I've got a body to bury."

"A body? Who?" Sarah June asked.

"Don't rightly know and don't much care." He looked at her closely. "You see anyone out in the woods? Someone who might have killed him?"

Sarah June shook her head.

"How about you ladies? Any of you see a gent nosing about?"

"Not carrying a shotgun," Tabitha said.

"The dead man was armed with the scatter gun," Slocum said. "Whoever killed him used a pistol. He never had a chance to use that." He tapped the shotgun barrel with the edge of the shovel blade. The sound rang out like a church bell pealing a death knell. The women flinched. Betty had been at the wagon when he rode up, but that didn't mean she wasn't the one who had dispatched the dead man. Wilhelmina was upset, and there was no telling where she had been. Her upset might be from squeezing a trigger and seeing a man die. Both Tabitha and Sarah June had been on the proper side of the road, but too much time had passed between the gunshot and when Slocum arrived for that to mean much.

"Why are you looking so strangely at us, Mr. Slocum?" Betty asked.

"Any of you packing a gun?"

The women exchanged looks and every last one of them

shook her head. It was about what Slocum had expected.
He might force the women to look at the body, but the reactions wouldn't mean much. If one had killed him, feign-
ing ignorance now would be easy, and the others would be
too distraught for him to decide what their reactions meant.
He had to admit it was possible none of them had killed the
man. They were entering dangerous territory, fraught with
road agents and down-on-their-luck miners willing to kill
for a meal or even the quarter of a dollar he had stuck into
his vest pocket.

Slocum doubted it was that simple an explanation for
the dead man.

"I'll bury him. Any of you want to say a prayer for him,
get to it."

"Will you be long?" Tabitha was pale but met his gaze
without flinching.

"You in a hurry?" Slocum asked.

"I think it would be of benefit to us all to put as much
distance between Salt Lake City and ourselves as possible."

Slocum again considered making them try to identify
the body.

"It might be one of your husbands," he said.

"You think one of us is capable of murder?" asked
Betty. "I never once considered killing my husband. I
loved him, in a way. What I wanted to get away from was
sharing him."

"I'll be back as quick as I can," Slocum said. "Pack up
and be ready to roll."

He hiked back into the forest and found a decent spot at
the edge of a glen, where he buried the man. If there had
been any chance the dead man was one of the women's
husbands, he would have insisted they all view the corpse.
The calluses on the dead man's hands showed he was more
likely a cowboy used to roping, not farming.

He finished tamping down the dirt in a mound; he
thought it might keep the coyotes and wolves from digging

it up for an easy meal. There ought to be rocks, but he would have done that only for a friend, not a man who had fired a shotgun in his direction.

As Slocum returned to the camp, he had a chance to study the women once more. Wilhelmina stood apart from the others, quietly sniffing and wiping at tears. Betty, Sarah June, and Tabitha huddled together as if they were sheep caught in a blizzard and needed to share body warmth. There was no telling what had happened.

Slocum tossed the shovel into the rear of the wagon, then climbed into the driver's box and said, "Let's get another ten miles along the road, ladies."

Three climbed into the back and Sarah June once more took her spot alongside him. But Slocum noted how quiet the once-talkative woman was. That suited him just fine. He needed some time to think through what he had gotten himself into, agreeing to deliver them to their prospective husbands.

4

Baxter Pass lay behind them, and Slocum watched the Twin Buttes to the north slowly get swallowed by a gathering storm. Lightning stabbed downward but no thunder sounded. The storm was still far away. But the gray clouds and the swift movement around the upper peaks told him that getting through the higher Douglas Pass some distance away—and all uphill—would be difficult. It was still early in the year for a major storm, but the Rockies were always treacherous.

He looked at the four women, all huddled together in the rear of the wagon, and wondered how treacherous they might be. Sarah June had remained beside him until they reached Baxter Pass and the sharp wind blowing down from the higher slopes had driven her back with the others. He missed the feel of her leg pressed against his, although she had never said anything more that gave him reason to think he might be able to sneak off with her and share warmth of a different sort.

Slocum had seen friendly women before, and they were usually charging for their favors. Sarah June was a different matter, being on the lookout for a husband. Still, Slocum was willing to fill in for whomever that might be until the pretty blonde woman found her heart's desire.

"You needing more blankets?" Slocum called. The wind picked up even more and cut at his lips, cheeks, and ears. The women were probably even colder, in spite of being out of the wind down in the wagon bed surrounded by their insulating chests of clothing.

"Could we stop, Mr. Slocum?" Tabitha asked. "I don't know how much longer I can stand this. I need a fire to warm myself."

Slocum looked at the road and then up to the Twin Buttes and the storm beginning to turn serious there. Putting in another few miles today might mean the difference between life and death. If they were caught between the two passes when a blizzard hit, they might be goners. For a second, Slocum even considered turning around and retreating through Baxter Pass to lower elevations where the storms weren't as likely to catch them. If he did that, though, it might be spring before they could push on toward the mining towns of the Book Plateau, where they intended to find the miners, who had already paid good money for their wives.

"The storm's coming in fast," he said. "If we don't go on, we might be snowed in for days."

"What's the difference between setting up camp here or a mile down the road?" Betty asked. "It's all the same."

It wasn't, but Slocum had no heart to argue the point. He saw that the other women agreed with Betty. Slocum shrugged and began looking for a decent camp, one where they might ride out the storm if it came their way and dumped as much as a foot of snow on their heads. He rounded a bend and smiled. Luck was still riding on his shoulder. All along the road he had seen line shacks constructed by other travelers. Ahead lay another. A small one. They would be cramped inside, but he doubted if the four women would care. He certainly wouldn't.

Slocum swung the wagon around behind the rickety shack and fastened the reins to the brake.

"Here we are. The finest hotel room in all the Rockies," he said.

"I'm glad you said 'room,'" Sarah June said. "You'd have been a liar if you'd said 'rooms.'"

"Carry what you'll need inside with you," Slocum said. "I'll hunt for some firewood."

"Wouldn't whoever built the shack have left some for us?" Wilhelmina seemed unaware of how ridiculous that sounded. Betty took the tall blonde aside and quietly explained.

"We'll help hunt for firewood," Tabitha said. She looked at Sarah June, who wasn't as inclined to join the search. The dubious warmth of the shack beckoned to her.

"That's all right. I can find enough to get a fire started," Slocum said. He wanted to scout the area to be certain that they were alone. Ever since the mysterious shotgun-toting rider had been murdered, Slocum had been wary of others along the road. They had passed three other parties, all coming out of Colorado and going into Utah. Not once had he seen anyone behind them on the trail riding in their direction.

The chance that someone paced them farther along the road was slim, but Slocum needed to put his fears to rest. The longer he rode with the women, the prettier they looked to him. He could hardly imagine what a prize any of the ladies would be to a lonely miner or trapper out in the mountains for the past six months.

He began scouring the area for firewood and found enough to last them the night. After delivering it to the ladies, he saw the flakes fluttering down from an increasingly cloudy sky and knew he had made the right decision to stop for the day. Before morning there would be a significant accumulation of snow on the ground. Another hour of gathering wood produced a stack waist high. He slipped into the cabin and pushed the door back into place. Leather hinges had long since rotted away.

"Feels good in here," he said, slapping his hands against his arms and moving closer to the fire built in the center of the shack. There was no stove. A firepit rimmed with rocks was hardly better than a campfire, and possibly worse since the smoke was already filling the cabin. He left the door open a crack to provide ventilation and then sank down beside the fire.

Sarah June handed him a steaming cup of coffee. He let it warm his hands a moment, then drank.

"Better than anything I could brew," he said.

"Boil, you mean," Betty said with disdain. "I've seen how you boil your coffee until it's strong enough to melt lead."

"Keeps me going," Slocum said. He stiffened as he felt something creeping up along the inside of his thigh. Cabins like this were always filthy with lice and even less desirable companions, but a quick glance down caused him to draw his legs closer together so the other women could not see how Sarah June was feeling him up.

Her fingers stroked and caressed and moved higher until he was getting uncomfortable. There was only so much room in his jeans, but she never stopped. Her clever fingers moved about until they pressed down over his burgeoning erection.

"You're sweating, John," Sarah June said. She grinned wickedly.

Slocum glanced at the other three women. Wilhelmina dozed in one corner. Betty and Tabitha argued over something, and he did not care what. Sarah June's hand was becoming more and more important to him.

"You shouldn't start what you can't finish," he said.

"Why not? We can go outside. For a spell. They won't care."

"In the snow?"

"Snow!" Sarah June's hand disappeared. She jumped to her feet and went to the door. Struggling, she pulled it back enough. "Look, everybody. It's snowing!"

Slocum was sorry he had mentioned it. While it would not have been as pleasant as some things he had in mind, having Sarah June stroking up and down his hardened length was mighty fine. Now her enthusiasm had been transferred to the heavy, wet flakes tumbling from the storm that had finally overtaken them.

"That means we're not going anywhere for a spell, doesn't it, Mr. Slocum?" asked Betty. "How long are we going to be stranded?"

"Can't rightly say. If the storm passes over fast, we can be on the road in the morning. From the look of it, though, I reckon we might be here a couple days. Getting through the next pass won't be easy, even without snow and ice on the road."

"Could be worse if it thaws," observed Tabitha. "Mud."

As cold as it was getting, Slocum doubted they would have to contend with that.

"Might as well get some grub and bed down for the night," he said.

"Bed down," murmured Sarah June. She smiled at him, that wicked twinkle in her eyes. The dancing light from the cooking fire illuminated her face and left the others hidden in shadow, but Slocum knew better than to pursue the thoughts running through the blonde's mind—and his cock. It was better than a week of travel after they got through Douglas Pass until they reached their destination, and the dissension among the other women would be too much to tolerate.

"Alone," he said softly so only Sarah June could hear. Her expression fell, then an elfin smile danced on her face. She set about spreading out her bedroll next to Slocum's. On his other side, Betty spread her blankets. Tabitha and Wilhelmina crowded close on either end. Even so, they were crowded in the tiny shack.

Slocum went to sleep with Sarah June's hand moving up and down on his manhood, but she would not allow him to run his hand under her skirts and explore more interesting territory.

For the night, that was all right.

"Another day," Slocum said, peering out at the knee-deep snow. It had snowed furiously all night, the wind whistling through the cabin as if the thin walls did not exist. The five of them had crowded closer and closer together until they slept in a big pile. Slocum did not object, although he wished there had been a little more privacy to share with Sarah June.

"We can't risk it today?" asked Betty. She appeared worried at the prospect of spending another night in the cabin.

"We have plenty of wood," Slocum said, "so we won't freeze."

"What about food? We'll run low if it snows even more and we're trapped," she said.

"You have a point," Slocum said. "Better if I go hunting for game now, rather than waiting for fresh snowfall. I can walk in this, even if we can't drive the wagon."

He pulled his Winchester out and made certain the action worked. It was not yet cold enough to freeze the oil. He slid the door to one side and let in a gust of icy air. Sarah June crowded close behind him and looked out past him.

"Want company?" she asked in a low voice.

"I'm going hunting," he said. "You'd scare the game away."

"Do I scare you?"

Slocum looked at her, then smiled crookedly. "I reckon you do."

"Then you should learn to face your fears and deal with them," she said. "Or maybe let them face away from you so you can sneak up on them from behind. I like it like that."

The other three women were beginning to grow restive because of the cold air blasting into the cabin. Slocum stepped out into the snow alone and helped Sarah June draw the door back into place. Her fingers lingered on his hand before the door flopped into place, leaving the women inside and him out in the bright, clean, cold air of the Rockies. Slocum made his way around to the side of the cabin, tended the animals, then began his hunt.

In weather like this, he might be able to bag a couple rabbits. They would still have their brown fur and stand out against the white snowbank. He might even get lucky and find a deer. Dressing down even a small one would provide plenty of food to take them to the other side of Douglas Pass.

Slocum took a few minutes to survey the area. The fresh layer of snow was untouched by human or animal. He made his way eastward along the road until he saw bear tracks. This made him hesitate. Killing a bear with only his carbine would be a chore. The huge animals were strong and tenacious. But the notion of a bear skin to keep him and Sarah June warm caused him to begin the hunt.

The saucer-sized paw print told him he was after a young bear. That would be better for him. It might take several accurate shots to bring down the bear, but if he had been up against a full-grown black bear, the chance of killing it would have been far less. He had once seen a hunter fire point-blank into a bear's face. The .44-caliber bullet had bounced off the bear's thick skull and infuriated it. Slocum had buried what was left after the bear had finished its gory feast.

The tracks led into a wooded area, then up to higher elevation. Slocum finally spotted the animal about midday, as it stood haunches-deep in a stream, big claws catching fish and tossing them to the bank for eating later. The bear was larger than a cub. Slocum considered not bothering with it, because he would never be able to carry all the meat back to the cabin in a single trip. In mountains like these, there was no point thinking anything he left behind would not be eaten by a half dozen different scavengers before he could return for it.

He eyed the fish on the bank and considered frightening

the bear away and stealing its catch. A dozen fish would cook up mighty fine and provide the food they'd need for another day or two. By then, the snow would have melted in the bright autumn sun.

As he considered how to get the fish, the bear turned, spotted him, and let out a bloodcurdling roar. Slocum brought his rifle to his shoulder. The range was only a couple dozen yards, but he wished he had a Sharps .50 or even a heavier caliber buffalo rifle. He thought the bear would lumber out of the stream, rise up on its rear legs, and then roar a bit before trotting off.

It charged.

He fired in reaction, his aim off. The bullet tore a chunk of flesh out of the bear's shoulder. Slocum saw fur and blood spray outward and knew he was in big trouble. He levered in another round and fired again. The bear was close enough now for him to see its bloodshot eyes. This round found a target in the bear's chest. From the way the bear staggered a little and made a funny coughing sound, Slocum knew he had drilled it through a lung. But that didn't stop it.

The bear might be dying, but it was not dead.

Six-inch claws raked at him. He fired with the bore of his rifle pressed against the bear's throat. This snapped the bear's head back and caused it to stumble. Dancing out of the way, Slocum got off three more shots before he was certain the bear was dead.

He sat in the snow and panted harshly. His breath left silvery trails from his nostrils and the sweat froze on his forehead, but Slocum was happy. He was alive and had enough bear meat to feed the five of them for several days.

He set about butchering the bear, taking only the choicest parts. Carrying more than thirty or forty pounds of meat was out of the question in the knee-deep snow, but he made certain he took the skin to wrap it all in. The skin would require curing, but it would make a mighty attractive rug. He made certain he took the paws, with their savage claws, and then added a half dozen fish to his load. The cold would keep any of it from spoiling on his way back to the cabin.

Slocum heaved the bear skin laden with the meat and fish over his shoulder and staggered. He might have kept too much of the carcass, but he was determined to return with as much as possible.

By nightfall the cabin was within sight, and he had only dropped ten pounds of the bear meat.

"Get the fire built," he called. "I've got plenty of meat to go around."

Slocum stumbled along a few more feet, then put down the load. Smoke trickled through the cracks in the cabin, but it was mighty quiet. He had expected the women to rush out to help him. Or at least Sarah June should have come outside to greet him.

He pulled his rifle around and made sure there was a round in the chamber as he advanced.

"Sarah June? Betty? Tabitha, Wilhelmina?" No answer.

He took a deep breath, then lowered his shoulder and shoved hard against the door. It creaked and then gave way as he forced himself into the shack. The women had braced firewood against the door.

"What's wrong?" Slocum demanded. He looked around. Three women huddled together on the far side of the cabin. "Where's Betty?"

"Th-they took her, John. They kidnapped her!" Sarah June came to him and threw her arms around him. "They took her! Don't let them get us, too!"

Sarah June began crying as she clung to him. Then he found himself surrounded. Both Tabitha and Wilhelmina were clinging fiercely to him, also.

All he had to do was figure out what had happened to Betty and everything would be perfect. Somehow, he doubted the answer to that question was going to suit him.

5

"What happened?"

"Sh-she was taken," Wilhelmina stammered out. "She goes for wood, gets kidnapped!"

Slocum looked to Tabitha and Sarah June for more information. Tabitha was closing into herself and would not even meet his eyes. He took Sarah June by the arm and got her to her feet.

"She was out looking for more wood. It was so cold in here," Sarah June said. There was a catch in her voice. She found strength to let out everything Slocum needed to know in a single rush. "I saw her, they didn't see me or they'd have nabbed me, too. Two men. Huge men dressed in shaggy fur coats."

"Mountain men," Slocum said. It was unusual for a mountain man to team with another, but the heyday of the Green River Rendezvous and making a decent living by trapping was long past. Times were hard enough that the reclusive men might have teamed up and taken partners simply to survive.

The notion of Betty being shared by two men who only saw civilized towns once or twice a year made Slocum go cold inside.

"They didn't see me," Sarah June said, "and I did nothing to keep them from taking her. They caught her neat as a pin. They came up from both sides, and she had nowhere to run."

"They're used to hunting dangerous game. Catching an unarmed woman would be simple for them," Slocum said. His mind raced. It was already past sundown and the temperature was plunging. Trying to track two mountain men in the dark would be hard. In such temperatures, it could be deadly. Then he thought what the men would do to Betty. They were little more than animals.

"How long ago did they take her?"

"An hour, maybe less."

"There's food," Slocum said. "Bear meat. Cook it up, if you want."

"I . . . we aren't hungry," Sarah June said.

Slocum did not press the point. The smell of cooking meat might be a strong attractor for the men. He was surprised that they had not already found the cabin and wagon, with its team. Or maybe they had. They might think only four women were responsible for driving the wagon and intended to pick them off one by one. Enjoy one, throw her away, and kidnap another until they were all used up—and dead.

"Here," Slocum said, thrusting the rifle into Sarah June's hands. "Can you use that?"

"Yes," she said in a small voice.

"Don't shoot me if I come back. And if Betty gets away and returns, don't shoot her."

"Know my target," Sarah June said, looking at him. "Shouldn't you keep the rifle? You can kill them from a distance."

"It won't work that way," Slocum said. The men would be in camp, probably with Betty close. In the dark the chances of him hitting her or missing them was too great. Whatever he did had to be done as close up as possible. If he could jam his Colt Navy into a belly and then fire, that would be the safest shot to take.

He bent and ran his fingers over the hilt of the knife sheathed in his boot top. Then he made certain his six-shooter was loaded.

"These will be enough," Slocum said.

"Come back, John," Sarah June said. She impulsively stood on tiptoe and kissed him full on the lips.

Slocum hardly noticed. His mind was already out in the snow fields, working on a scheme to sneak up on men who lived by their wits in dangerous territory. He left without a word, but he noticed the woman's scent lingered for several paces, until he began following Betty's tracks in the snow. He looked up at the sky and saw that the clouds had cleared. That made it likely it would get even colder, but he needed the starlight to illuminate his search.

Betty had made no effort to hide her tracks. Why should she? If anything, it gave her an easy means to find her way back to the shack when she didn't know the terrain. Within ten minutes Slocum realized how easy it would be to get lost. The snow covered most landmarks he would normally use for navigation. The tracks curved toward a wooded area. Slocum grew wary when he spotted another set of tracks. Starlight caused the ridges to gleam like molten silver. He reconstructed the scene. That had to be where Sarah June had been, watching Betty.

It took Slocum less than a minute to find the other two sets of tracks. Sarah June had reported accurately what had happened. Betty was still slogging toward the woods to hunt for firewood when the two men, both wearing moccasins, had swooped in to grab her. The snow was all tamped down and mud below showed how Betty had struggled. The long strides of the men approaching and the shorter ones leaving showed how they had rushed her and how, after catching the woman, they had fought to hang on to her.

Along the way Slocum found bits of fur from the mountain men's clothing. Betty was fighting for her life. A strand of brunette hair that must have been the woman's showed that one man held on to her hair to control her. Slocum followed at a rapid pace because the mud beneath the churned-up snow had not yet frozen. With the temperature dropping fast, that meant they had come this way recently. Slocum had no good idea about how accurate Sarah June had been at guessing when Betty had been taken. She might have beaten him to the shack by only minutes.

Slocum's nostrils flared when he smelled pinewood burning. A fire ahead warned him he was nearing the men's camp. He stood stock-still and listened. A fitful wind blew through the snowcapped trees, but the snow muted the sound. He heard laughter and turned slowly until it was directly in front of him. The tracks he followed did not go in that direction, but they might have had their hands full with Betty. Slocum had to admit the woman would be more than a handful—she would be quite an armful.

He struck out directly for the sound. The starlight intensified and lit the ground to an almost dawn brightness. Slocum pressed on until he reached a gap in the trees and saw a curl of smoke lazily reaching for the sky. He followed the smoke down to earth, where two lean-tos were fixed against trees, the fire and three figures between them. From the dark silhouettes, Slocum figured the one on the right was a mountain man, but the other two were closer to the same size. He was glad he had not brought the rifle. Taking out the larger man might have let the other mountain man kill Betty.

Moving like a ghost, Slocum flitted from tree to tree. The snow crunched under his boots and occasionally a sucking sounded as he pulled free from clinging mud, but he was skilled enough to get close to the men. His eyes widened. He was even happier that he had not brought the rifle. The largest of the three turned out to be Betty, laden with heavy blankets against the cold. The two men wanted to keep her warm and alive. If he had assumed the largest was a kidnapper, he would have shot Betty by mistake.

"Me, Grubstake, me! I get to go first."

"Shut yer tater trap. We bin over this, Kennard. You remember what we decided last time?"

"You cheated, Grubstake. You cheated. Them cards was marked."

"You're a damn fool," the one Slocum pegged to be Grubstake snarled. The mountain man stood and shoved his companion, who rolled like a puppy dog and came to his feet. A knife flashed in the dim firelight.

Slocum saw this to be his best chance to rescue Betty. He didn't know if she was bound, but he suspected they had her hogtied some way to keep from having to chase after her repeatedly.

While the other two squabbled and then began to tussle, rolling around in the snow, Slocum made his move. He reached Betty's side in a few seconds and pressed his finger to his lips to keep her quiet. To his relief, she nodded. There was no panic in her brown eyes.

He slid his knife from its boot sheath and slashed through the rawhide strips they had used to bind her ankles. She moaned as the tight bands were cut.

"My feet are numb," she whispered. "They tied them damn tight!"

Slocum took her arm and steered her back in the direction he had come. Leaving tracks in the snow was unavoidable. Getting back to the shack with Betty hobbling along painfully would be a miracle. Slocum knew these experienced frontiersmen would be on them in a flash. He suspected they already knew every detail of the women in the shack and had been intent on working down through them one at a time. Whether they had counted on Slocum was something he would have to learn.

"Get on back," Slocum said. "Find the tracks in the snow and follow them."

"What are you going to do?"

He pulled her down into shadows at the edge of the stand of trees.

"No time to talk. I have to get rid of both of them. They won't let you go easily. It's not in their nature."

"You'll kill them?"

Slocum did not answer. He saw the set to Betty's jaw and the way she shook all over. He wasn't sure if it was from cold or pure rage.

"I want to do it. I want to cut their damn throats myself!"

"No time to argue the point," Slocum said. He saw the two men still rolling about, but one had gotten his legs wrapped around the other and came up on top. He moved quickly for a schoolboy pin. "Might not have to do much," he said, seeing the mountain man grab his partner's head and begin banging it against the ground. "They might kill each other."

"One'll be left," Betty said. "I want him!"

He looked her square in the eye and had to laugh. He admired her spunk. Betty glowered at him, and then a tiny smile crept onto her lips. She was laughing soon, too.

"You're right, John," she said. "I'll be a good girl and go back to the others."

"Keep them from getting too rambunctious," Slocum said. "Be careful, also; I left my rifle with Sarah June."

"I won't sneak up on them." Betty started to fade into the forest, stopped, and came back. She dropped to her knees in front of him.

"What is it?" he asked, thinking she had seen something to bring her back. Her answer startled him. She reached out, grabbed him by the ears, and pulled his face to hers for a nice, long kiss. She finally broke it off, licked her lips seductively, then silently got to her feet and vanished into the darkness. Slocum touched his lips. He wondered if Sarah June would mind sharing him with Betty.

Then he pushed such notions from his mind. He had

some serious convincing to do, and it wouldn't be as easy as shooting the bear had been.

He made his way back to the lean-tos and saw only the dark shape of the fallen mountain man on the ground. The other was nowhere to be seen. Slocum cursed under his breath, then made his way Indian style to see what condition the man was in. Blood trickled from the fallen man's mouth, but his chest heaved up and down in a steady rhythm. His partner hadn't killed him. Slocum was considering doing just that when he heard a roar of rage and looked over his shoulder.

Where the other man had gone, Slocum did not know or much care. But the mountain man had returned now and found his captive missing. Slocum knew what the man's first thought would be—recapture Betty. Slocum shot to his feet and laughed as loud as he could. This got the man's attention.

"Lose something, you sorry son of a bitch?" Slocum laughed harder, to rub salt into the wound. Then he lit out across the field as fast as he could plow through the knee-deep snow. He had not scouted this part of the mountainside but had a good idea what he was searching for. He angled downslope and then across the bottom of the snowy meadow. Bluffs began poking up on his left. Mostly he saw nothing but dark rock on the sheer face, but ahead he found what he wanted. A vast snow field stretched up the side of the hill.

"Come back and fight, you miserable wart," cried the mountain man hot on his trail. Slocum saw that the man was catching up. All he had to do was follow Slocum's tracks, and he did not have to plow through the snow if he stayed in Slocum's footprints. Slocum touched the butt of his pistol, exhaled sharply, and then plowed on through the snow until he reached the spot where he could make a stand.

"You shouldn't kidnap innocent women," Slocum taunted. "You'll come to a sorry end."

"She wasn't bein' used by nobody."

"Are you Grubstake?" Slocum saw how this stopped the mountain man in his tracks.

"How'd you come to know my name? I never met you 'fore."

"Everybody in Colorado knows about a man called Grubstake," Slocum said.

"Do tell? I never knowed I was famous."

Slocum used the byplay to regain his breath and position himself a little better. He found a big boulder and maneuvered until Grubstake was in the clearing.

"Yeah, everybody tells how dumb you are." Slocum needed the mountain man to come a little farther. And he did. There was no way any self-respecting man could tolerate Slocum's insults. With a roar that started deep in his barrel chest and rose up like some unstoppable force of nature, Grubstake bellowed and came forward.

Slocum stepped out, six-shooter in hand.

"That little peashooter ain't gonna stop me!"

"No?" Slocum shifted aim from the mountain man to a tree halfway up the side of the snowy mountainside. He fired. The tree shivered and dropped a considerable amount of snow to the ground. Not enough. Slocum fired again. Grubstake came closer, bent on vengeance. Slocum considered changing his tactics and seeing if he could drop the bull of a man. He decided he could risk one more shot uphill.

This one broke loose the packed snowbank and started an avalanche.

Grubstake saw he was caught in the middle of an exposed, steeply sloping area. He let out a cry that was more what Slocum would expect from a stepped-on dog. Then the white tide washed over the mountain man, picking him up and carrying him off as if he were no more than a flea on a dog's back.

Slocum felt no triumph knowing the avalanche he had caused would sweep Grubstake over a cliff some distance downhill. The man had sealed his own fate by kidnapping Betty. The ground stopped rumbling under his feet, but Slocum still waited behind his sheltering boulder. There had not been enough of a snowfall to send the avalanche over him, too, but the bulk of the huge rock reassured him.

Looking around the edge, he saw some small streams of snow still flowing down from higher elevations. It might be hours before the last of the snow quieted down into a stable field again, but Slocum had no time to waste. He made his way across the occasional tumbles of snow and got to the far side. He had a long walk across the meadow once more, and he found himself growing more tired with every step he took. But the starlight shone brightly and gave him the sense that he was hiking in daylight. No time to sleep. He kept up his forced march until he got back to the mountain men's camp.

For a moment, he tried to figure out what was wrong. The fire still burned cheerily. The lean-tos were undisturbed. Then he spun around and looked behind him.

Kennard was no longer flat on his back in the snow. Slocum took a few quick steps to make certain he was not missing the man due to shifting light caused by clouds crossing the sky.

"Damn," he muttered. The ground was too cut up with frequent crossings for him to tell where Kennard must have gone, but Slocum thought he knew. He spun and plunged into the woods where Betty had retreated.

It took him less than a minute to see Betty on her knees. Her hands were behind her back. She looked up and made a curious choking sound. Slocum started forward, knife out to cut her bonds, but when he got close enough he saw why she was making such peculiar noises.

Kennard had tied a strip of rawhide with cruel force across her mouth as a gag. Betty looked up, real fear in her eyes. She tossed her head and looked behind Slocum.

Too late.

The blow knocked Slocum to his hands and knees. His knife went flying and his head felt as if it would explode as he tried to keep from passing out. All that kept him conscious was the mocking laughter that built his anger.

Then even this receded as a second blow knocked him facedown into the snow.

6

"Lemme think. Should I jist cut yer damn throat so you'd bleed out in the snow, or maybe I kin do somethin' fun with you?"

Slocum knew Kennard was talking about him, but he could not move. His arms and legs were paralyzed. He rubbed his cheek into the snow and felt the cold sting. Bit by bit his strength returned. Slocum lifted his head enough to see Betty still on her knees and bound. Her eyes were fixed on him. Her look of desolation changed to hope when she saw he was awake. Slocum was not sure he had ever been unconscious, but the heavy blows to the back of his skull had stunned him. He hoped Kennard was sure he had knocked him out.

Slocum shook his head to signal Betty not to do anything. Slocum took inventory. His knife lay some distance away, but his Colt Navy was still in its holster. Lying on his belly, though, made it hard to draw and fire. Worse, he felt mud all along his belly and upper thighs. The Colt was a precision instrument and if it got dirty, it refused to work. Slocum spent long hours while on the trail keeping dust and grit from the workings of the six-shooter. He might roll over, draw, and try to fire, only to find the six-gun clogged or jammed.

He would last about a single heartbeat before Kennard was on him, his hunting knife flashing across Slocum's throat.

Slocum began to inch his legs up and turn slightly onto his right side so his holster was out of the muck. From the sucking noises, he knew he was covered in freezing mud. Without any choice, he swung over. His hand flashed for the ebony butt of his pistol. He drew and the gun slipped from his grip. The combination of mud and cold had turned his fingers too feeble and slick to properly hang on to the six-shooter.

The sounds brought Kennard up from where he had hunkered down, cutting at something on the ground with his knife. A smile brought his lips up into a sneer.

"Yer back among the livin', eh? Good. Now I kin kill you all properlike."

Kennard reared up like a grizzly, the hunting knife flashing in his grip. Slocum wasn't able to get a good look at him because of new clouds scudding across the sky and obscuring the diamond-hard points of the stars. Slocum grabbed for his fallen gun, not sure where it had gone. By rolling onto his side for it, he saved his own life.

Kennard's heavy knife made a dull *thunk* as it drove hilt-deep into the ground where Slocum had been only an instant before. Slocum kept rolling until he came to his knees. He tried to drag out his six-gun but found himself bowled over as Kennard slammed into him. Arms around the bulky mountain man, Slocum fought to get a good grip. The furs Kennard wore were greasy—almost as greasy as the man's skin. Try as he might, Slocum failed to get a grip adequate for fighting.

He found himself under the heavy man's knees, pinned securely.

Slocum saw the man fumbling to pull free another knife sheathed at his belt. What had happened to the first one was anyone's guess. It must have fallen from the mountain man's grip during the scuffle. But this one was firmly in his fist. Slocum saw Kennard's arm lift. The occasional light from the stars caught on the shiny silver blade as it paused at the top of a thrust. Slocum heaved with all his strength and caused Kennard to shift his weight. And then he went flying away.

Betty had gotten to her feet, put her head down, and charged full tilt into Kennard. Her shoulder caught him in the armpit, forcing him to not only drop the knife but also to leave his superior position atop Slocum.

"Run, John, run. Get away," Betty cried out. How she had cut the rawhide gag, Slocum didn't know. Unless she had chewed through it like some wild animal. From the ferocious look on her lovely face, Slocum could believe that. She kicked and pummeled Kennard, keeping him off balance.

Slocum got to his feet and found his six-shooter. He knew the instant he leveled it that it could not fire. Mud dripped from the barrel. One shot and it would blow up in his hand. Slocum had seen men with clogged barrels lose their hands and, in one case, a life. Fragments from the barrel would fly in all directions like a cannonball landing in the midst of an infantry position.

He crammed the gun back into his cross-draw holster and hunted for the knife Kennard had dropped. He was still a little woozy from being knocked down, but he saw silver on the ground and pounced on it. Only Kennard got there first. Slocum found himself pressing down into the bucking, writhing mountain man.

"Gonna kill you," Kennard squalled. "I ain't lettin' nobody come 'tween me and her."

Slocum tried to get his arm around the man's throat. He was tossed off. Landing hard in a snowbank, Slocum lay stunned. He stared at the clouds coming in and irrationally worried about getting trapped in another snowstorm.

Again he would have died except Betty kept up her assault. She rose from the ground and flung herself forward, tangling Kennard's legs. The mountain man toppled forward.

"Run," she cried. "Get help. He can't do much to me."

Slocum moaned as he crushed more snow beneath him, getting to his hands and knees. He was no quitter, but Kennard was stronger, fresher, and more focused at the moment. Slocum still could not leave the woman to the mountain man's lust.

Kennard scrambled over Betty and tried to get his footing in the snow and mud. Slocum saw his chance and took it. He shoved hard, catching Kennard on the shoulder. The man slipped and slid, off balance, and then went rolling down a small incline.

"Come on," Slocum said, getting his arm around Betty and pulling her to her feet.

"You can't leave him," Betty panted harshly. "He'll follow us to the ends of the earth. You, he'll kill. What he'll do to me will be worse."

"I know," Slocum said. "That's why we're getting the hell out of here."

"But I can't run, not like this," Betty said, indicating how her hands were still tied behind her back.

Slocum knew there was no time to free her. He heard huffing and puffing like a steam engine behind them. Kennard had fought his way back up the slope and was coming after them again.

"There," Slocum said, "we can hide over there."

"Hide? He can see our tracks in the snow. There's no way—" Betty gasped when Slocum shoved her forward toward a crevice in the rock face. The mountainside was covered with snow, but Slocum saw right away there was no hope of duplicating an avalanche like the one that had carried away Grubstake. Even if he had had a pistol ready to shoot, there was not enough snow here.

Betty gave a loud cry and vanished suddenly from sight as Slocum pushed her in. Slocum looked back in the direction of Kennard struggling along behind them. The man moved with the implacable force of a storm blowing down from the higher elevations. Nothing short of death was going to stop him.

Slocum looked back to be sure Betty was safe. Then he saw that he had shoved her into a crevice seemingly without a bottom. He poked his head forward and saw movement almost ten feet below.

"Are you all right?"

"I can hardly breathe," Betty gasped out. "That was too big a fall for me."

"Anything broken?"

"No."

Slocum wasted no time. He swung his feet around, let them dangle into space for an instant, then dropped. He tried to hang on with his fingers, gripping the edge of a rock. The frozen rock and his slippery fingers betrayed him. He landed atop Betty, much to her sputtering and cursing. Forcing himself to one side, Slocum sat in the mud and peered up at the crevice. Only a thin sliver of sky was visible, and that was rapidly being shut off by building clouds. Another snowstorm might drop a fresh white blanket before morning.

He tried to decide if they could weather the storm there, if Kennard might find and come after them, or if they had fallen into a trap where they would eventually die.

"Come on," Slocum said, pulling Betty to her feet. "We have to explore."

"Wouldn't do having him see us, that's for certain," Betty said.

Slocum walked her a dozen feet along the narrow crevice until he found that they were trapped in this direction. He reversed course and went in the other. As they passed under the hole where they had fallen, Slocum saw Kennard sticking his head down.

"I'll kill you. I'll kill you both! But her, her I'll have fun with first. Mark my words!"

Slocum reached for his pistol, then remembered it was out of action until he cleaned it. Shooting Kennard would be easy. The man made no effort to hide himself.

"Come on," Slocum whispered to Betty. "He might not be able to see us." As if putting the lie to his words, Kennard began dropping rocks on their heads. Slocum worked his way through a narrowing in the crevice and then popped out on the far side into a tunnel that wound around.

"Is this a mine?" Betty asked. "And when are you going to get my hands free?"

"When we're safe," Slocum said. They had found the way out. Not ten yards off he saw starlight reflecting off bright snow. He tried to keep his bearings, but the way they had twisted around underground confused him. He needed to see the mountains and stars to get reoriented.

"He's not going to . . ." Betty's words trailed off when the opening was suddenly blocked by a huge body.

"You're in there, ain't ya? I kin smell you!"

"Stay behind me," Slocum said. "I don't think he can see us in the dark."

He began edging forward. Kennard vented a constant stream of curses but did not move from his post blocking their escape. Slocum hefted a rock, pressed against the cold stone wall of the crevice, and got within five feet of the mountain man before Kennard heard him.

With a roar, Kennard grabbed for him. Slocum lifted the rock and brought it crashing down on the man's wrist. In the dark he missed connecting solidly, but he took away a little skin and sent a shower of blood spewing forth.

With this small victory came instant defeat. Kennard might have one injured hand but his other was still as strong as ever. He grabbed Slocum by the coat lapels and yanked. Catapulted from the crevice, Slocum tumbled over Kennard's shoulder and rolled downhill a few yards. When he slammed hard into a rock, he was dizzy and unable to get his feet under him.

"You jist don't wanna die, do you?" Kennard came downhill, knife swinging. Slocum blinked, thinking he was going blind, but it was only a light snowfall giving a bizarre aspect to the attacking man. Slocum got to his feet but was still half bent over when Kennard hit him at a full run.

The impact lifted Slocum off his feet and sent him rolling fast downhill. He felt every rock he hit until his head grazed a boulder. Then he was only vaguely aware of the world filled with falling snow and raging mountain men.

"I ain't puttin' up with you no more," Kennard declared. Slocum felt himself rolling faster. He tried to stop himself but only jerked his arms and legs around to the point of damaging his joints. Changing his tactics, he pulled his arms in close to his body to protect his face and head. This kept him from being knocked out entirely.

He came to a halt against a dead tree trunk. He lay stunned for several seconds. In the distance he heard Kennard coming for him and knew it was death to remain where he was. But his legs refused to obey. His arms were bruised and curiously weak. Most of all his head spun in wild, crazy circles. Slocum heard wild cries but could not figure out who was responsible. Some were high-pitched enough to come from Betty, but they could as easily be from Kennard.

"Got you now, you miserable li'l wart," Kennard said. There was no confusing this with anything Betty might be saying. Slocum pushed to hands and knees and caught a foot in the gut, driving the wind from his lungs.

"I reckon you done kilt Grubstake. Ain't no loss. I git his share of ever'thin'," Kennard said. Slocum felt himself flopped onto his back and his hands being pulled toward the nighttime sky. It took him a few seconds to realize that Kennard was securely tying his wrists with more rawhide strips. By the time he fought the bonds on his hands, Kennard had turned his attention to Slocum's ankles. A new loop of rawhide circled his feet, making certain he was completely hobbled and helpless.

"Fight like a man," Slocum got out. His mouth had filled with cotton and his tongue must have been the size of a German sausage. He kicked, but with his feet bound together there wasn't a lot of force. He swung his balled fists, but Kennard easily avoided him. Slocum was as weak as a kitten after the beating he had received.

"Cain't unnerstand you, but then I don't have to now. I figure you're going to fly real good all trussed up like that."

"Fly?"

"You don't know we're standin' on the edge of a big cliff? We are!"

Kennard dragged Slocum to his feet and held him so he could see downward into blackness. From the distant sound of rushing water, a river made its way down the valley. They stood on the rim of a steep precipice. Slocum could not even guess how far it was to the bottom, but it would be more than enough to ensure his death. He fought, kicking out. Kennard held him like a rag doll.

"Over the side with you, you pain in the ass!"

Slocum prepared to die, only to hear Betty cry out. She attacked Kennard again, driving the mountain man to his knees. Slocum stumbled but could not get away.

"I'll kill you, I will," raged Betty. She hit the ground hard and writhed about, coming up next to Slocum.

"Here," she said urgently. "Take it!"

Something hard pressed into his hands. He gripped it only to feel his feet lifted from the ground again. This time Kennard grunted as he flung Slocum out into space to his death.

7

Slocum let out a throat-tearing scream as he sailed through the air and plunged downward into emptiness. Another scream ripped from his lips as he came to a sudden stop upside down and slammed hard into the rocky face of the cliff.

Clinging fiercely to the knife Betty had shoved into his hands before Kennard had thrown him out into space, Slocum fought to make sense of what had happened. He finally worked through the bigger facts, ignoring details until his life wasn't in danger. He hung upside down. Somehow the rawhide strip Kennard had used to tie his ankles had looped over a rock outcrop jutting from the cliff side. This had not only kept him from falling to his death, it had swung him back under the lip of the cliff, out of Kennard's sight.

With the good came the bad. Slocum was upside down. His head felt as if it would explode as blood rushed into it. He wasn't sure whether blood trickled from one ear, but that was a detail. He held up the knife and stared at it. Straining, he tried to flip the knife around to cut the bonds on his wrists. That proved impossible without dropping the knife. When a wind began blowing along the canyon, which was cut by the roaring river below, Slocum swung gently. He felt the rawhide strip around his ankles begin to stretch—soon it would break.

Turning frantic, he worked to cut the bonds on his wrists but could not reverse the knife without dropping it. If that happened, he was a goner.

Inspiration hit him. Slocum crammed the knife handle down under his gun belt so the sharp side of the blade was up. Tensing his belly tightened the gun belt against the knife handle even more. He began sawing. The knife was not as sharp as it should have been. Slocum cursed the lazy mountain man for not dragging it over a whetstone more often. As he gasped and panted, the knife slipped from his belt. Slocum almost doubled up to force the knife back under his belt.

His belly ached and his wrists were cut from the rawhide strip. As his blood soaked into it, it would harden and probably begin to contract. This goaded Slocum to work harder, but he knew he had to work more methodically. He caught the tip of the knife under the rawhide and slowly moved down until he was sure the knife wasn't going to slip out from under his belt again or turn. It took several more strokes, but the rawhide finally parted.

Slocum could not help himself. He let out another cry of pain as circulation returned to his deadened hands. Worse, the wind was whipping up, causing him to swing to and fro like the pendulum in a Regulator clock. Slocum held back any more outcry, then rubbed his hands together until he was certain he would not drop the knife. It was his lifeline.

Gripping the handle firmly with one hand, Slocum grabbed his pant leg with the other, trying to inch upward so he could cut the rawhide strip around his ankles. His strength petered out before he could succeed. He flopped back. Then he realized how lucky he had been. If he had cut the only thing keeping him from falling, he would have died.

Swaying in the increasingly chilly wind, Slocum thought hard. He finally flipped the knife around so he could use it for stabbing. Twisting toward the cliff face, he saw a crevice the knife blade might fit into. He thrust out and drove the blade securely into the tiny crevice. Using the knife as a handhold, he pulled himself around until he could grab a nearby rock. Hurriedly working the knife free, he repeated the maneuver until he took the pressure off his legs. He forced them down and pulled up and turned and struggled and finally worked himself around to sit on a narrow rock ledge. Only then did he cut the strap binding his feet.

Again relief flooded over him. Slocum had to fight to keep from falling off the narrow ledge. Taking a longer time than he liked to get his strength back, he was finally ready to find a way back to the top of the cliff—and Kennard. He had a powerful big score to settle with the mountain man.

He got his feet up on the ledge, then stood. Occasional gusts of wind threatened to tear him away from his aerie, but Slocum moved with great deliberation, finding secure toeholds and handholds until he planted both elbows on the rim. Poking his head up, he looked around. All he saw was a sea of white. The wind was blowing the snow about, erasing old footprints. With a huge heave and his feet kicking fast and hard like he was riding one of those bicycle contraptions, he slithered away from the edge of the cliff and lay in the snow and mud.

"Kennard," he muttered over and over, focusing his anger and hatred to give himself strength. When he got to his feet, the blunt knife with a chipped blade in his hand, he was ready to tangle with a pack of wildcats.

But Kennard would do for a start.

The wind was blowing harder now, forcing Slocum to pull up his bandanna to protect his nose and lips. Before he located the tracks of Betty and Kennard heading back toward the camp where the lean-tos were still pitched, the soft wet flakes turned into hard snow pellets and hammered at his eyes. Slocum plunged on through the increasing storm, knowing what Betty's fate would be if he did not reach her quickly enough.

She had saved his life by grabbing the knife and pressing it into his hands. It was his turn to save hers.

His first hint that he approached the camp was the faint flicker of a fire. Kennard had not built it up too high, so the wind wouldn't whip the flames about. Most of the heat would be lost to the storm in any case. Slocum doubted Kennard intended to depend much on the fire for warmth when he had Betty to keep him warm all night long.

First he saw the faint fire. Then he heard a woman's shrieks over the rising wind. Slocum wanted to rush forward but forced himself to hang back and reconnoiter. He remembered how he had been wrong before and would have shot Betty rather than either Grubstake or Kennard. This was no time to make a similar mistake. He would get only one chance to strike. He was weak and his hands shook. His vision was blurred, and if he had to walk more than a mile farther, he would simply collapse.

He was at the end of his rope. He had to be sure Kennard was at the end of his life.

"Don't go makin' me mad, girlie," Kennard's voice came. The lean-tos had been repitched so they were together. Slocum approached from the blind spot. He saw faint shadows on the canvas. One was larger; that was Kennard. He knew it because the other figure was bare to the waist and cast the most delectable female shadow possible. Slocum could even see the outline of the woman's breasts.

When Kennard made a grab for Betty, Slocum moved around the canvas sheet. The woman's eyes went wide as she recoiled from Kennard. She had been fighting him off, but something about the way she reacted now alerted the mountain man that trouble had found him. Again.

Kennard shoved Betty away and rolled back, fumbling

for a pistol. Slocum pounced on him like a hunting mountain lion. He brought the knife down with all his strength into the middle of the man's chest. Slocum thought he had hit a rib from the way the shock went all the way up into his shoulder. Then he realized Kennard carried something in an inner pocket that had deflected the blade away from his vile heart.

"John, John!" Betty's outcry confused Kennard for a valuable instant. He looked back at her as she grabbed for the pistol in his hand.

Slocum yanked the knife back, found a new spot, and then drove the blade downward with what little strength remained in his body. Again he felt resistance. Then the resistance disappeared and he drove the knife entirely into the mountain man's chest.

"Sumbidge," Kennard grated out. "You done kilt me."

It was not apparent to Slocum that was what had happened. Kennard was still fighting. For a few more seconds. He reared up like a bear and grappled with Slocum. They tumbled out into the snowstorm, and then Kennard lay motionless atop Slocum.

"Don't shoot, don't shoot," Slocum called to Betty. The sight of the woman, naked to the waist, shivering in the cold, and holding a six-shooter with both hands, was alternately provocative and frightening. She could not hope to hit anything she aimed at with her hands shaking so badly.

Slocum heaved Kennard away and lay for a moment, gasping for breath. A new weight pinned him down. It was Betty. She fell on him, her mouth kissing his hungrily.

"Gotta get under cover. Freeze," Slocum got out.

"It's all right now, John. It'll be all right. The bastard is dead! You killed him."

"Yeah, I did," Slocum said. He sat up and stared at the body already disappearing under a thin white blanket of snow. "I want to see something." On hands and knees he went to Kennard and ripped open the man's coat. He kept working down, layer after layer, until he came to the pocket directly over the man's heart. He pulled out a small Bible.

"It didn't save him," Betty said. She clung to Slocum. The snow was landing on her shoulders and exposed breasts, melting from her body heat, and then refreezing almost instantly.

"Might save us," Slocum said, putting the blood-stained Bible into his coat pocket. He put his arm around Betty and guided her back to the lean-tos. He saw right away they would never be able to weather the growing storm here.

"Get dressed. We've got to get back to the shack."

"There's no way you can make it, John. You're white as a sheet."

"Feel half past dead, too," Slocum said, recognizing truth in the woman's words. "Caves. Back where he tried to throw me over."

"Uphill from there? Where we found the crevice?"

"Yes, there," Slocum said. He gathered what he could of Kennard's belongings. The mountain man had wasted no time picking through his former partner's equipment and adding it to his own. Slocum slung the rucksack holding it all over his shoulder. He staggered under the weight.

"What of the tarps?"

"Leave 'em," Slocum said. As much as he would have liked to have the heavy canvas sheets, it would take too long to free them from their supporting poles.

"Like hell," Betty said. She forced her way through the snow to Kennard's body and pulled the knife from the man's chest. She wasted no time slashing at the canvas, cutting it loose from where it had been carefully bound to a pair of sturdy limbs. She rolled it up, tucked the knife under her coat, and grabbed Slocum's arm. "Move," she ordered.

"Yes, ma'am," he said. Slocum gathered strength as they returned to the rocky face of the mountain, but he still depended on Betty to steady him at times.

They found a cave, its mouth dark and narrow. This

suited Slocum because he was in no condition to fight a grizzly bear for space in its lair. Whatever might be in the cave already—fox or even wolf—would be more easily evicted. He stopped in the mouth and took a deep whiff. Nothing but biting cold air cut into his nostrils. He forced his way into the cave and sank down a few feet inside.

"Here," Betty said, unrolling the tarp the mountain men had used in their lean-tos. She dropped a blanket down and quickly lay beside Slocum.

"Fire, need a fire."

"How do we hope to start it in this wind?"

Slocum silently held up the Bible. They hurriedly scrounged enough wood for a decent fire that would see them through the night. It took three books from the Bible before Slocum had a roaring fire that lit the interior of the cave.

"Satisfied?" Betty demanded.

"Not yet," he said, pulling her close. They sank down to the tarp, then worked the blanket around themselves. He felt the hammering of her heart as she crushed close to him, sharing body heat. Slocum listened to the whistle of the wind outside as the blizzard raged, but the sound of Betty's breathing slowing until she fell into a deep sleep soothed him more. Soon enough, he followed her into sleep.

Slocum awoke to utter silence. The world was cold and quiet. He poked his head up a little and saw that the mouth of the cave was half filled with snow and beyond, the world was beautiful and cold. At least a foot of snow had fallen during the night.

As he moved, so did Betty. She murmured softly and snuggled closer. He sank back. There was nowhere to go until they shoveled the snow out of the cave mouth, and it was mighty relaxing lying alongside such a lovely woman. The brunette started moving her hand, and Slocum was less relaxed and more aroused. She slid her hand under his shirt and stroked across his chest. He winced a little, but she kept stroking, her fingers twirling up little spires of his chest hair. And then she slipped down lower, under his belt, down to his crotch.

He was suddenly not relaxed at all.

Slocum wondered if Betty was still asleep and dreaming of being in bed with her husband. Then she put that notion to rest.

"You've got something I want, John," she said. Her fingers circled his erection and began squeezing gently, rhythmically, getting the feel of his hardness.

"Are you sure?"

"Of course I am," she said in her acid way. She softened her tone a little and said, "It's only right, me giving you a reward for risking your life like you did to save me."

"You don't have to," he said.

"Of course not. I want to. And you want me to," she said. Her fingers tensed around his fleshy stalk until he was downright uncomfortable. She moved around, keeping him in hand, and unbuttoned his jeans so she could drag out his hardened length. Before he could say a word about how good that felt, she showed him what pleasure could be like. Her lips closed on the tip of his cock, then began tonguing and licking and softly kissing.

Pulses of fire radiated down into his loins. Slocum was hardly aware of lifting his hips off the cold rock floor and trying to shove himself deeper into that loving mouth. She took a couple inches and then backed off. She cradled him with her tongue and began bobbing her head up and down. The warmth, the sucking, the way she used her lips and teeth and tongue all excited him more and more.

He felt like a young buck with his first woman.

"I . . . I don't know how long I can hang on," he said. "That mouth of yours is mighty educated."

"Do tell," she said, letting him pop free so she could

look up into his eyes. Her brown eyes were pools of lust that mirrored his own. "What you gonna do about it?"

Slocum smiled, reached down, and drew her up so she lay across him. His ribs hurt, and he didn't have a muscle that failed to protest. Then all that faded away as their mouths met in a fierce kiss. He ran his hands down Betty's sides and cupped her ass, pulling her down into him. He felt his hard shaft crushed down by her weight, but he was in the right place—only separated by the woman's skirt.

"Here," she said, putting her knees on either side of his hips and rising up enough so she could unbutton her blouse. Her luscious breasts came tumbling out. The nipples were already hard. Whether it was from the cold or anticipation of what was to come, Slocum neither knew nor cared. He reared up and took her right breast in his mouth, laving it with his tongue and then lightly nipping at it. Betty moaned softly and thrust her chest forward so he could take more of that tempting treat into his mouth.

He did. More and more of the soft, succulent flesh entered his mouth until he pressed down the hard nub with his tongue and gently chewed all around. Then he suddenly abandoned it and raced to the other, giving it identical treatment. If he had wondered whether it was the cold or himself that caused such rigidity in her nipples, this answered the question. He felt the throb of her heart accelerate as he pressed her nipple down farther and farther. The gasps and moans coming from her convinced him she was as excited as he was.

"Get those skirts out of the way," Slocum said. He reached down and grabbed a handful of cloth on either side of her hips and began pulling upward. Betty had to help. She wiggled and finally got the skirt bunched up around her waist, leaving her exposed.

"Mighty cold out there," she said. "Why don't you get inside where it's nice and warm?"

She lifted her hips, positioned Slocum under her, and then sank down, taking him balls deep into her molten core.

It was Slocum's turn to gasp.

"Hurting you?" she asked, barely able to speak.

"Not warm in there, hot. Damned hot. And wet." He ran his hands around and grabbed a double handful of her buttocks. Squeezing and kneading, he pulled and pushed and then began guiding her in the rhythm he desired most.

She rose to the point where only the plum tip of his cock remained within her trembling nether lips, then sank down slowly. Every inch was delightful torture for Slocum. The heat spread throughout his groin, his belly, his body. Knowing that she was not going to stop, he reached up and grabbed her breasts. He squeezed and kneaded and rotated them as she began moving faster.

"Oh, John, it . . . it's better than I thought," Betty cried out. Her eyes were closed and her head was tipped back, letting her long brown hair fall down her back. Then she began bucking and thrashing around, hips rotating and inner muscles clutching fiercely at Slocum's buried length.

Betty let out a cry that was part gasp and part animal howl. Slocum felt the hot tide rising within him, and when she clutched down on him like a mine shaft collapsing, there was no holding back. He jetted his seed into her molten center.

"Oh," she said, sinking down. She gave a couple quick inner squeezes, but Slocum was melting within her like an icicle in the spring sun. Betty smiled and then repositioned herself, still atop him. Her naked breasts pressed into his chest, and he felt her hot breath against his cheek.

"So good," she said. "Like I knew it would be."

"I can do better," Slocum said. "Right now, I'm all bunged up."

"Is that what you call it?" She laughed softly and began running her tongue around his ear. She said hotly, "I want more bunging."

Slocum surprised himself and responded to her with admirable speed. They spent the rest of the day in the cave, until it became too cold and Slocum had to go find firewood. The early evening showed a clear sky free of storm clouds in any direction. They would have to get back to the shack and the other three women in the morning.

But they had the night together.

8

"There," Slocum said with some satisfaction as he pushed the last of the frozen snow from the cave mouth. He squinted as the glare off the snow blinded him. He sucked in a deep breath and winced. His ribs were still sore from the pounding he had taken, and most every muscle in his body ached, too. But he felt nice and warm at the crotch because of Betty's careful ministrations. He had liked her looks from when he had first set eyes on her, but he had not realized she was as talented as she was. She would make some miner a mighty fine wife.

And the man she had married in Utah was a damned fool for choosing any of his other wives over her.

"Mighty cold," Betty said. She shivered, although she had a blanket pulled around her shoulders. "Can we walk in that snow?"

"Don't think it will be a big problem if we go slow. It looks wet enough to crush down a few inches and then support our weight. You just follow in my footsteps."

"I'll follow you anywhere, John."

This gave him pause. He didn't want the brunette getting attached to him. He had rescued her from the two mountain men, but he was not husband material. Not like she wanted.

"Was it that bad?" he asked. "In Utah?"

The chattering of her teeth stopped as she clamped her jaws together angrily.

"It was awful. No matter what I did, I was never good enough."

"I find that mighty hard to believe," Slocum said, smiling.

She had to laugh, too. "He told me the others were better in bed. They were better cooks. They were better housekeepers. They tended the children better."

"It was his way of keeping you in line," Slocum said.

"When I figured that out for myself, I left. I found that Tabitha and Wilhelmina were also less than satisfied with sharing their husbands. That's when we lit out and became outlaws."

This took Slocum aback for a moment, then he had to nod. By church law, the women would be criminals. They had broken their matrimonial vows, but Slocum hardly counted that as being a real felony. Getting them into Colorado was a chore he found himself liking more and more, men like Grubstake and Kennard notwithstanding. Then he remembered the other man he had come across on the highway—the one wielding the shotgun.

Someone had murdered him, and Slocum didn't know who it might have been.

"You know the other women pretty well, then?"

"Not really. We found ourselves fugitives for the same reason."

"Just Tabitha and Wilhelmina? What about Sarah June?"

"She joined up just as we made our deal with Preen to get us to a mining camp in Colorado."

"So you really didn't know one another until you decided to light out?"

"That's right. Why are you asking, John?"

"No reason," he said, but the dead man back on the trail bothered him. He understood Grubstake and Kennard. He was similar to them in too many ways, but the other man?

Why had he followed? None of the women seemed to have recognized him. So why was he killed? And who pulled the trigger? For all that, Slocum had not found the gun that killed him.

"When can we get back to the others? I want to push on."

Slocum looked at Betty and wondered what she really meant. There was a wistfulness in her tone that told him she wanted to stay here—with him.

"It won't take us long to get back. An hour or two at the outside," Slocum said, wondering if he was being too optimistic. He was still hurting all over, but once he got moving and warmed up his cold muscles, the trip would go faster. Betty could keep up without much effort since he would be carrying the pack he had taken from the mountain men's camp. They had eaten some of the grub in it, what hadn't been too maggot-infested. Neither Kennard nor Grubstake had been too fussy about what they ate.

"Let's get moving, then," Betty said. This time her words were as brittle as the beauty outside the cave. She had expected him to say something else.

"Got my duty to the others," Slocum said, but he got no reply. He tumbled into the snow and the crust broke under his weight. He got to his feet and slung the rucksack. Already he felt the cold working into his boots. Time to move and keep moving.

He helped Betty from the cave. She still clung to the blanket around her shoulders. Walking with it would be a chore, but Slocum said nothing. Let her figure how best to sling it around her shoulders. He had the feeling that if he bossed her too much, she would fly off the handle.

The glare caused him to squint constantly, but the bright sun put a lie to any more storms. Slocum chose his spots to step as carefully as possible. Most of the time he sank to mid-calf, but he kept on moving, no matter how tiring this was. Betty trailed him, stepping into his footprints. For her the going was easier. She still complained.

"Don't take such big strides," she called. "I can hardly jump from one to the next."

"Strike out on your own, then," Slocum said. They were not making as good a progress as he had hoped. It took more than an hour for them to cross the meadow and cut into the woods. Once there, the going was easier. Most of the snow still clung to the limbs above them. Betty complained even more now, though, of being tired and wanting to rest.

"We can rest with a fire warming us when we get to the shack," he told her.

"I can't go on much longer. I'm thirsty and I'm hungry and my feet feel like they're frozen through and through."

"Then we should speed up," Slocum said. "The sooner we reach the shack—"

"The sooner we get to eat and push on through the pass. Is there any chance we can make it, John? Really? The road would be all snowed over and icy. If the wagon slid off the road when we were near one of those long drops . . ."

"Then we'd die," Slocum said, not mincing words. He wanted to get back to the others, not because spending time on the trail with Betty was so onerous but because he had to think of the trouble the trio could get into. They were not experienced enough to survive long without his help.

"You don't have to be so rude about it."

"Dead's dead," he said. Slocum stopped for a moment and got his bearings. The Twin Buttes were crystal clear in the bright Colorado air and gave him a precise location he remembered well.

"How much farther?"

"Less than a mile," he said. "I can make out the road."

"Is that what those lumps are?" Betty said sarcastically.

"I can see the shack," he said. His voice was low. Betty let out a whoop of glee and sped up, but Slocum worried now. There was no smoke curling up out of the shack to show that the women had kept the fire going. If they had not posted a guard at night to watch the fire and to feed it, they might have all three slept—and frozen to death.

Ten minutes longer brought them to the shack.

"Wilhelmina!" shouted Betty. "Sarah June! Tabitha! We're back. We made it back!"

She struggled to move the door aside and get into the shack, but Slocum knew what she would find inside.

"They're gone! John, they aren't here."

"The wagon and team's gone, too." Slocum cursed under his breath. His horse was also missing.

"What happened to them? Those two mountain men?"

"Dead," Slocum said.

"Maybe not them. There might be others," Betty said. Slocum saw tears forming in the corners of her brown eyes, but the tears never spilled. It was too cold for that. She hastily brushed them away and left tracks of snow behind on her cheeks.

"There wouldn't be any others. Kennard and Grubstake would have run them off. They thought of all this as their land like a wild animal finds its range and protects it to the death." As he explained to Betty how mountain men thought, he walked around the exterior of the shack, trying to make some sense of the tracks he found.

"But were they kidnapped? They wouldn't have just up and left us, would they?"

"You tell me," Slocum said. "You know them better than I do."

"I don't know them hardly at all. I told you that. What happened to them?"

"They left us," Slocum said harshly. "There aren't any tracks other than theirs. From the way the snow is compressed, they left this morning after the snowfall. That means they can't be more than a few hours ahead of us. Did any of them know how to handle a team?"

"I doubt it," Betty said. "I don't. There's no reason they

would know how to handle farm animals other than to milk cows or tend chickens. Plowing was men's work."

Slocum dropped the rucksack by the door of the shack. "Then get started on some women's work. Fix us a hot meal. There's still firewood inside you can use."

"But kindling. I'd need—"

"Here," Slocum said, pulling Kennard's Bible out of his pocket. He had already used a portion of the pages to start their fire in the cave. "Put this to some use."

Betty took it and shook her head. She laughed ruefully. "I was always told it would be my salvation. Reckon they were right."

Slocum saw that her good humor was slowly returning. While she fixed food for them, including enough coffee to warm him all the way down to his toes, Slocum hiked to the top of a nearby hill. Shielding his eyes against the glare of the sun off the snow, he followed the tracks as far as he could. He thought there would be a good chance that the three women would have retraced their way to Baxter Pass, but they were pushing on. He nodded at this. It was smarter going on, even if they did not know the terrain, than to retreat.

He slipped and slid down the hill to the shack when the cooking aromas reached his nostrils. He took a deep breath, closed his eyes, and for a moment was transported back to Calhoun, Georgia, and his ma fixing their noon meal. The illusion vanished when Betty called.

"Come and get it or I'll eat it all myself!"

He joined her. The inside of the shack felt positively tropical in comparison to the exterior. She had done a good job with their limited supplies. If anything, she might have gone a little overboard because it would take some time catching up with the wagon.

"How long?"

Slocum blinked. It was as if Betty had been reading his

mind. Or was there anything else for him to be thinking about?

"A couple hours. I couldn't see them, and there's almost two miles of road visible. How much beyond that they've gone, I can't say."

"Why'd they leave us?"

"Reckon that's a question to get answered when we catch up with them. Right now, it's you and me."

Slocum saw Betty look up sharply. Their eyes locked. Slocum knew they could spend another couple hours quite pleasurably if he only made a move in that direction. If their situation had not been so desperate, he might have decided to linger. But they needed food, and he was worried about the three inexperienced women driving along an icy road in the Rockies.

"We're a team," Betty said without much conviction. Slocum knew a moment had passed, and he had disappointed her. That seemed less important than getting back on the road.

"The going will be easier now. We can follow the wagon tracks."

"The snow'll be crushed down," she agreed. Betty pulled the blanket tighter around herself and finished eating in silence.

Slocum packed what he could, warmed his hands one last time at the fire, then kicked snow on it to extinguish the flames. Rucksack in place, he started tramping along in the right-hand rut. Betty silently began walking in the left. Slocum found himself wanting to talk and yet needing to think about what he had gotten himself into. Taking the money from Preen for delivering the four mail-order brides had been necessary to pay off his debt to Jenks, but the chore was turning into something more than he expected. He cast a quick sideways glance at the brunette, who stoically marched along, trailing the blanket now so that it dragged in the wet snow.

Betty was pretty and she was certainly expert when it came to lovemaking, but Slocum had trouble with the notion that she was not only running from one husband back in Salt Lake City but going to another in a mining camp in Colorado. Either way, she ought to have been off-limits to him. Still, he considered what had happened between them in the cave as his due. He had rescued her from the mountain men, and that was not covered in the fifty dollars Preen had paid him.

"John!" Betty pointed.

Slocum nodded. He had seen the wooden sign pointing downhill. A narrow route branched from the bigger road, spiraling downward to a small community.

"Must be a mining town. That where you want to go? Braden?"

"No, no, we're supposed to go to Aurum," Betty said.

"Aurum? Do tell." Slocum had not bothered to ask, thinking he would find out when they got to the far side of Douglas Pass.

"What's so strange about that? Do you know something about Aurum that we don't?"

"No need to get your dander up," Slocum said, wondering at Betty's attitude. "Just a coincidence. A friend of mine's in Aurum."

"So you were going there?"

"That's about the only way I'm likely to collect from my friend. He owes me a few dollars." Even as he spoke, Slocum pressed his hand into his vest pocket where he usually carried his money. His fingers, numb as they were, traced out the shapes of two coins. One was a silver dollar. The other was a one-bit piece. Not much to keep him going after he parted company with the women and no longer had their supplies to rely on to keep his belly full.

"Small world," Betty said. "What about that town there?"

"Hasn't been anybody going to it since the snowfall," Slocum said. "And the wagon tracks go on, so we go on."

Betty nodded, as if this revealed some arcane truth, although she was reluctant. He did not blame her. The lure of a town was a hot meal, a warm bath, and maybe a solid roof overhead at night. However, this was not likely to be a prosperous town, caught as it was between the two passes, and might even have become a ghost town, as so many boomtowns did overnight.

They hiked on for another mile, but Slocum began to think he had made a mistake not seeing if Braden was able to offer some shelter. It had been crystal clear all day, but the afternoon brought new storm clouds at the highest elevations. It took very little for those clouds to slide down the slopes and deliver more snow. Being caught out on the road was not something Slocum hankered to do.

"There," he called to Betty. He heaved a sigh of relief. "I see them."

"Where? Where? I don't—oh, yes, there they are!" Betty jumped up and down with glee and clapped her hands.

Slocum saw the wagon through pine trees. The road switched back and went lower on the far side. He considered hiking along the road, and then decided to take the shortcut directly through the woods.

"Come on," Slocum said. "We can cut off a good twenty minutes of walking."

"All right. That makes sense since we can see them. Shouldn't you shoot your gun or something so they'd see us and stop?"

Slocum touched the butt of his six-shooter and remembered that he had not cleaned it when he had the chance back at the shack. The lure of hot food and a warming fire had driven it from his mind. Coupled with the worry about the three women pressing on without them, he had good excuses for not cleaning his Colt. That still did not make the fact any easier to swallow now that he needed it.

"Don't want to scare them," Slocum said. He plunged into the forest and found the going easier. Snow still clung to the branches above. In less than ten minutes they emerged on the far side behind the women in the wagon.

"Hello!" Betty called. "Wait up! We're here!"

Slocum saw Sarah June turn in the driver's box. She jammed on the brake and tugged hard on the reins to slow the oxen. The wagon had not been rolling along too fast, and she got it halted within a few yards. Slocum knew he had arrived at exactly the right time. Going downhill the way Sarah June had been would have caused the wagon to roll right on over the oxen. This was the first big downslope since leaving the shack and required special skills from the driver.

"Betty!" Both Wilhelmina and Tabitha piled out of the wagon and ran to embrace Betty. Sarah June paid them no attention. Her eyes were fixed on Slocum like a hungry mountain lion that hasn't eaten in a week.

"Good thing we caught up. Why'd you take off like that?" Slocum asked Sarah June.

"The storms worried us," the blonde said. "If we stayed, we were afraid we might get stranded."

"But it was all right to strand us?"

"You caught up. We knew you could, John," Sarah June said. "What kept you?"

"That's a long story," Slocum said. He looked up at the sky and began to worry even more. There was only an hour of daylight left, and the storm might engulf them if they pressed on.

"We need to find a level spot to camp," Sarah June said. Then she followed the line of Slocum's gaze. "Will it be a bad one?"

"Could be," Slocum said. "We'd be better off back at the mining town."

"Town? What town?"

"There was a signpost. Braden." From Sarah June's blank expression, he saw that she had missed the turnoff completely.

"Do you think we should go back?"

"I do," Slocum said, the wind whipping against his face. "Everybody in. We're heading for Braden."

"What? Where's that?" asked Tabitha.

"Tell 'em," Slocum said to Betty. He maneuvered the oxen around, a few feet at a time, until they were reluctantly pulling the fully loaded wagon back up the slope in the direction of the turnoff.

Slocum heard Betty detailing their adventure, then felt Sarah June go rigid beside him on the driver's bench when Betty went into far too much detail about the night she and Slocum had spent in the cave. If Betty wanted to count coup, she was doing a fine job. It certainly soured Sarah June mighty fast.

"There it is," Slocum said. "See the sign? Braden." He wanted to cut off Betty's chatter. "We'll have a hotel to sleep in tonight."

"Won't need too many rooms, I suppose," Sarah June said acidly. "One for Wilhelmina, Tabitha, and me, and another for you and Betty."

"It's not like that," Slocum said, wondering why he bothered to explain to Sarah June or the others. Keeping peace among the women was not part of his job. More than this, he had enjoyed the time with Betty and would be tempted to do it again, should the opportunity arise.

"What should I care?"

"Nothing," Slocum said to Sarah June. She sat with her shoulders squared, staring ahead as if she could penetrate the gathering twilight with her fierce gaze.

Slocum guided the wagon down the increasingly steep hill, thinking he would have to lock the front wheels at any instant. When the slope was nearing that point, the road leveled out and Braden was fully visible in a hollow at the base of the hill. Slocum had almost hoped the town would be abandoned, but enough of the buildings had smoke curling from chimneys to tell him at least a hundred people lived and worked there.

"Where's the hotel?" asked Tabitha, with ill grace.

"We might have to stay in the livery stables," Slocum said, but as the words escaped his lips he saw the run-down hotel. He doubted Braden got much through traffic other than prospectors hunting for gold and the miners on their way to stake out and work claims. Anyone living in Braden would have their own house. Or shack, from the look of the place. He had seen prosperous towns and towns down on their luck. Braden was somewhat less well-off rather than down on its luck.

The women had spotted the hotel and were already vaulting over the side to land in the slush.

"Looks like it'll get mighty cold tonight," Slocum said, wiping a few snowflakes off his nose.

"Got that way earlier," Sarah June said. Then she jumped to the ground and hurried to join the other women. Slocum noted how three of them clustered together and crowded Betty out as they made their way into the lobby. Slocum touched the silver dollar in his pocket and decided it was not worth it to him to stay in that fleabag of a hotel.

He got the oxen pulling toward the livery and gratefully got out of the hard bench seat. He rubbed his hindquarters, sore from both the pounding along the road and the long trek overtaking the wagon.

"You need some space inside, mister?" the stableman called out. "Lookin' like another storm's a-brewin'."

"I wouldn't bet against that," Slocum said. "Don't have much in the way of money to pay, though."

"Might be we kin swap fer some stuff," the stableman said, poking through the wagon. "My wife's always gnawin' at me like I was some kinda bone to git her fancy duds."

Slocum started to tell the man he would have to deal with the four women, then he shrugged it off.

"Any two items," Slocum said, "in exchange for stall space for my horse and fodder for all the animals."

"That's mighty generous. You got a deal. And you kin

poke around in the straw until you find a comfy spot to curl up in, too."

Slocum ate a meal out of the supplies he had taken off the mountain men, then did what he could to tend the animals. Before he drifted off to sleep, he made certain his six-shooter was clean and ready for action. Then he spread his blanket in a stall so he could stare out the window above him. A white curve of snow had already accumulated and more continued to fall. The snow blanketed both the ground and noise around, letting Slocum drift off to a much-needed sleep.

Until he was shaken so hard he came fully awake, his hand on his Colt Navy.

"Sarah June," he said, staring at the distraught woman. "What's wrong? What time is it?"

"It's almost dawn," Sarah June said. "And it's Tabitha."

"Tabitha?"

"She's missing. Kidnapped, John. Somebody snuck into our room and grabbed her not five minutes ago!"

9

A million thoughts flashed through Slocum's head, but all of them were confusing.

"Tabitha? Not Betty?"

"What? Her? No," Sarah June said with distaste. She backed away from Slocum as if mention of the other woman reminded her how much she hated him at the moment. Yet she had come to him.

"You woke me out of a sound sleep. Explain what's going on."

"Come to the hotel. The others can tell you. Well, Wilhelmina can. She and Tabitha were sharing a room."

Slocum got his boots on and then strapped his cross-draw holster around his waist. He was glad he had cleaned his pistol now. There was a good chance he would have to use it. Remembering the fights with Grubstake and Kennard made him silently vow to shoot first and then use a knife in any fight.

He pulled his coat around him when he stepped from the cozy stables into the falling snow. It was almost warm until the snowflakes landing on his face and hands melted and turned to ice. Slocum pulled his hat down against the storm and trudged along after Sarah June. She had come out into the dawn without so much as a coat. Her dress was getting wet from the snow, molding to her body in a delightful fashion that Slocum knew he had better not comment on. Otherwise, he might be on the receiving end of a barbed comment or worse. Sarah June might take a swing at him. She had the look of a real brawler when she got riled.

In the shabby hotel lobby were already gathered Betty and Wilhelmina. They sat side by side on a settee. Whatever bad blood had existed between them because of Betty sleeping with him was all gone. They held one another and tried not to cry.

"Oh, John, she's gone. They took her!" Betty cried openly now. Tears ran down her cheeks and turned her brown eyes bloodshot.

"Who? Did you see who kidnapped her?"

"N-no. We were asleep."

"Wait, wait," Slocum said. He tried to get it all straight in his head and knew he was doing a piss-poor job of it. "Start from when you checked in to the hotel. Don't leave out anything."

"We came in," Wilhelmina said. "The clerk is an old man. He hardly noticed we were women." She spoke with certainty. Slocum doubted any man could have failed to miss Wilhelmina's willowy body and decidedly feminine form unless he was dead, but he said nothing. "We went to our rooms."

"Yes," cut in Sarah June. "Tabitha, Wilhelmina, and Betty were all in one. There wasn't another room fit for a human. I found a cot and pitched it at the far end of the hall."

Slocum stared at her in disbelief.

"By opening a door I had some privacy," Sarah June said haughtily. "Besides, who was likely to see me?"

"There wasn't any room with us," Betty said. "Two in the bed and I was on the floor next to it. There wasn't any more room there."

"So you were on the floor? Who stepped over you to get to Tabitha?"

"I . . . I don't know," Betty said, crying harder now. "I should have seen them, but I didn't. I was so tired!"

"We all were," Slocum said. To Sarah June, he asked, "Did you hear or see anything out in the hall?"

"I heard footsteps. That was what woke me up. I went to check on them and there was an empty spot in the bed. Tabitha was gone. Somebody stole her away!"

"Looks like that," Slocum said. He stared out the window in the front door. The snow was slacking off. It would be dawn in another thirty minutes. "Where's the clerk?"

"Follow the snores," Sarah June said coldly. "I doubt anything less than a mine explosion would wake him."

Slocum got the old man awake. Rheumy eyes tried to focus on Slocum, then the man reached for false teeth he kept in a glass of water beside him. He fitted them in, rubbed his eyes some, then got around to asking, "You want a room, mister? We're all full up."

"One of your boarders is missing. A tall woman, dark hair with streaks of gray. Somebody spirited her out of her room."

"Ain't got a room, mister. Maybe tomorrow," the old man said, louder now. Slocum realized that the clerk was deaf as a post, in addition to being half blind and needing store-bought teeth.

"Who might be looking for a woman around Braden?" Slocum almost shouted. This got the old man's attention.

"Danged near ever' last man in town. Ain't more'n five women within twenty miles of the town, and there's close to a hundred miners in these hills workin' claims. What makes it worse, none of them wimmen's whores. All wives."

Slocum remembered the stableman's swap for tending the oxen and the horse. He must be one of the lucky men with a wife.

"Who'd be most likely to kidnap a woman?"

"Cain't remember all their names—and I mean *all*, mister. Ever' last one of 'em'd do it, if they thought they could git by with it. And they might. Ain't had a marshal in town ever. Sheriff's been by once in the past two years. But we git by."

"Go back to sleep, old-timer," Slocum said. He returned to the three women, all clustered together now, feud forgotten.

"Did you find out anything, John?" asked Sarah June.

"I'll need to go hunting," he said tiredly. "I'll be back as soon as I can."

"With Tabitha?"

"With her," Slocum agreed, but at the moment the odds looked mighty slim on finding her. Going from one miner to the next looking to see if lace curtains had been put up in their line shacks hardly amounted to a reasonable way to find Tabitha. Whoever had taken her would keep her tied up for a week or two, until any chance of someone finding her was past. With the snow falling the way it was, the miner might not even have to tie her. The threat of freezing to death might be greater than her distaste for wherever she had ended up.

"Find her, John. Please." Betty threw her arms around him. Slocum responded awkwardly, then found himself engulfed by Sarah June and Wilhelmina, too. This was a sight better, but he finally disentangled himself and left, wondering if he had made a promise he could never keep.

Slocum saddled his horse and set off just as people began stirring in town. He had to hurry. The way into town along the road showed only their faint wagon tracks from dusk the day before. Almost three inches of snow had fallen. Enough to leave tracks but not enough to hide a trail.

He hoped.

Circling Braden gave him one distinct set of tracks going out of town. Wagon tracks. These being the only ones he had found, he gave his horse its head to follow. He fell into the rhythm of riding easily and dozed off in the saddle for more than a few minutes at a time. When the snow began fluttering down again, he snapped awake. Slocum pulled up his bandanna to protect his face from the elements and looked around. The road the wagon followed turned and corkscrewed itself higher onto a mountainside. Dotted on the hill were tailings from a dozen mines. Slocum doubted any of them were still producing gold ore—if any of them ever had.

He touched his six-shooter to reassure himself, then started up the steep hill. He knew what he would find at the top: another mountain man or grizzled prospector with no respect for women. See a pretty one and snatch her. One reason so many miners fit in well out on the frontier in communities like Braden was their lack of social graces.

His horse struggled as the way became steeper. Slocum dismounted and walked, wondering how the miner had ever driven a wagon up this hill. When he heard the distant braying of mules, he got his answer. The sure-footed, powerful animals could climb up a sheer cliff, given the time and enough carrots and sugar cubes to keep them happy.

Some distance from the mules, Slocum tethered his horse. He walked the rest of the way, turning a bend in the road and seeing a mining shack with a wisp of smoke coming out a stovepipe. Behind the shack was a rude corral holding four mules. Slocum wondered if the miner had struck it rich. That many animals took some feeding—and they were almost worth their weight in gold in a place like Braden.

Slocum slid his pistol from its holster as he approached the door of the shack. He might knock or he could kick in the door. Either way had advantages. Instead, Slocum tugged at the latch. Open. Carefully sliding it up, he put his shoulder to the door and gently opened it. The heat blasting from the interior was enough to stagger him.

Then he swung in, six-shooter leveled.

It pointed at a man sitting at a table, forking in a plate of beans. The miner, hardly twenty from his looks and maybe still wet behind the ears, looked up in surprise.

"You're welcome to share my grub, mister. You don't have to shoot me to get it."

He had a pleasant voice and sounded educated. Slocum looked around. A small shelf over the cot in the far corner held a dozen books.

Seeing Slocum's interest, the man said, "I got a degree in geology from Harvard. That's in Massachusetts. Back East."

"I know where it is," Slocum said. "What I want to know is where you've got Tabitha."

"Tabitha? You—you're not—?" The man stood, kicking his chair away.

"I am," Slocum said, aiming his six-gun straight at the man's chest.

"Mr. Smith, you don't own her. You—"

"Hold your horses," Slocum said. "My name's not Smith. What gave you that idea?"

"You're not Tabitha's husband?"

"Far from it," Slocum said.

"Then why are you waving that hogleg around? Put it down. Now!"

The sharp snap of command in the man's voice might have affected another man, but Slocum had spent too long in the CSA, listening to damn fool officers issue commands that would get their men killed. His gun hand never wavered.

"Where is she?" Slocum asked. "The next time I put that question to you and you don't answer, I'll shoot."

"Go on. You'll never take her back!"

"Where is she?" Slocum cocked his six-gun and pointed it straight at the man's head. The young miner turned white and closed his eyes but never flinched.

"You put that gun down this instant, Mr. Slocum!"

Slocum glanced over his shoulder and saw Tabitha holding a bundle of greens.

"You all right?" he asked.

"Put that gun down," Tabitha repeated. "Of course I am fine. Why shouldn't I be?"

"He kidnapped you, that's why,"

Both of them gasped, then laughed. Tabitha pushed past where Slocum stood in the doorway and put the greens she had collected on the table before hugging the miner tightly.

"Edwin didn't kidnap me. I went with him. Willingly. We're going to get married as soon as the circuit judge makes his rounds in the spring."

"You scared the other women something fierce," Slocum said. "You could have told them you were leaving."

"I left a note. On my pillow. I detailed how you should leave my chest at the stable and that Edwin and I would return for it later. This load was too heavy to possibly bring all my belongings."

She pointed to the cot where a single valise stood open. From what Slocum could see inside, it was not Edwin's.

"Reckon I made a mistake," Slocum said. He watched Tabitha closely to be sure the miner wasn't holding something over her. From the way she hugged him so tightly, it might have been the other way around. She had set her cap for Edwin and snared him.

"Could I have a word with you, Tabitha? In private?"

"There's nothing I want to hide from Edwin."

"It's about your trip to Aurum."

"He knows," Tabitha said. Her dark eyes shone defiantly.

"Well, seems to me you took money under false pretenses. There's some gent waiting for his mail-order bride in Aurum and he's not going to get you."

"How much?" Edwin asked.

"How much what?" For a moment Slocum was confused.

"The man in Aurum paid one hundred dollars for me," Tabitha said.

"Did each of them pay the same?" Slocum did a quick sum in his head. Preen had made out like a bandit. Four hundred dollars. He had not paid one hundred for the oxen and wagon, hardly that for the supplies, and another fifty for Slocum's services. That left Preen some hundred and fifty dollars for doing nothing more than writing an ad and sending a few letters.

"I'll give you the money," Edwin said. "You can pay off whoever it was that wanted my Tabitha, so he won't be out any money."

"Just a bride. He might get testy about that, whether he loses money or not."

"I'll make it a hundred and fifty," Edwin said.

"This claim must be mighty good for you," Slocum observed. Edwin said nothing, but the way Tabitha hugged the miner even tighter told the story. Edwin had struck it rich on one of the few mines in the region that actually gave up its gold.

"I told you I was a trained geologist. The instant I saw the outcropping I knew there was gold here. And there was."

"Now there's gold and me," Tabitha said.

Slocum holstered his pistol and shook his head. "There's no reason for me to complain. I'll get the best deal I can for you and send anything left back."

"Keep it for your troubles," Edwin said. He looked at Tabitha, who mouthed "John Slocum." "Keep it for your troubles, Mr. Slocum."

"Can't complain about not having to fight you for her," Slocum said.

Edwin then hastily explained what had happened with Tabitha. "She came willingly. We met at the Braden mercantile, and I took her to dinner. I proposed and she said she would let me know. I never thought she would find me in the middle of the night." The way Edwin blushed told Slocum how Tabitha had found him to seal their pact.

"I ought to get back to town," Slocum said. "The other women will be worrying."

"John," Tabitha said, looking out into the darkness, "might be better for you to stay the night. It's looking like a new storm is brewing."

Slocum thought about the offer for a moment, then shook his head. "That's mighty kind of you, but I have to get back." The last thing he wanted was to intrude on their wedding night. Getting back to Braden would not be much of a problem as long as there wasn't a full-fledged blizzard. He doubted that would happen this early in the season, especially after the goodly amount of snow that had already fallen. The clouds would be exhausted for some time to come.

"You know best, John," Tabitha said.

Edwin handed him a small leather bag and said, "That ought to be about right. I could use my scales but—"

"I'm sure it will be fine," Slocum said, growing increasingly uncomfortable being here because of the way the two looked at each other. He tucked the bag of gold dust away before the pair could rip their clothes off and begin rutting like animals in front of him.

"A cup of coffee to warm you," Tabitha offered.

This Slocum took. He drank so fast it scalded his mouth and tongue, and then he said his good-byes and left the cabin fast. Outside in the cold mountain air, he shivered as sweat began to freeze on him. It had been hot inside. He grinned crookedly, knowing it would get even hotter before the sun came up the next day.

He took a few minutes to go to the mouth of the mine. He peered in. The shoring was precise and the tracks into the mine were free of rust and had been laid with the same precision shown in shoring up the rock. He picked up a rock and examined it. Not seeing it well enough, he lit a lucifer and peered at it.

"I'll be damned. He did hit a mother lode." Slocum started to toss the rock back onto the heap, then tucked it into his pocket. It would be worth five dollars or more, if all the sparkle he saw was real gold. He had no doubt that it was.

Tabitha had landed herself a man destined to be rich. A young, educated man, to boot.

Slocum carefully made his way downhill to where he had left his horse. The twilight had faded and the stars were trying valiantly to pierce the clouds. The best he could tell, there was not going to be another big storm before he returned to town. The few fitful snowflakes falling didn't seem to have enough heart to build to a real snowstorm.

He swung into the saddle and started back down the steep road when he drew rein and stopped to listen. Hard. Something was not right. Slocum almost shrugged it off as nerves when the gunshot rang out.

A second report echoed downhill from the direction of Edwin and Tabitha's love nest. When a third shot sounded, Slocum turned his pony's face and started back up the hill for the cabin, dreading what he would find.

10

Slocum had no idea what he was riding into. The darkness cloaked the mine site, but the foot-long tongues of orange flame lashing outward showed at least two men were firing—into the shack. When no return fire came, Slocum knew that Edwin and Tabitha had to be in serious trouble.

He whipped out his six-shooter and took careful aim as he skidded to a halt. His sights centered just above the spot where he had seen the muzzle flash. How far off the gunman was, Slocum could not tell. He squeezed the trigger, and his trusty six-shooter bucked in his hand. He heard a yelp of pain and saw a new muzzle flash, this time directed into the ground. He had done more than wing the man. He might have hit him smack in the chest.

"Claude, you hit? Did they git you?"

Slocum homed in on the call, knowing it could be a trick to get him to expose himself. He jumped from horseback and let his pony trot out of the way. He could always run the horse down later—if he came out of the gunfight able to ride. Slocum listened and heard the crunch of boots against the newly fallen snow. It was in the approximate direction of the second muzzle flash. Slocum fired three times, one left, one right, and one round in between. He heard a startled cry. He doubted the gunman was as seriously injured as his partner, Claude, but anything that slowed them down was worthwhile.

Hunkering down beside the shack, Slocum reloaded his spent chambers. He scanned the night for movement. Nothing. He edged around to the other side of the shack and waited. His patience outlasted that of one of the owlhoots coming to the shack. For the briefest instant, the man silhouetted himself against the night sky. Slocum fired three rounds. He was certain one had struck the man in the leg, but there had not been a loud response, as there had been before.

Rather than advance to see what damage he had caused, Slocum rapped on the shack door and whispered, "It's me, Slocum. Are you all right in there?"

"John?"

"It's me, Tabitha. Let me in."

"He's wounded, John. They shot him."

"Who are they?" Slocum duckwalked into the shack. From the light arrowing through holes in the wall, the men outside had simply opened fire, hoping to kill anyone inside.

Slocum blinked when he saw Tabitha. She was naked to the waist. It didn't take much imagination to guess what she and Edwin had been doing when the bullets started flying. Slocum was glad that he had skedaddled when he had. The woman had gotten naked and was undoubtedly under her husband-to-be when the first bullet came through the wall.

"Here. You know about these things. How is he?"

Edwin was naked below the waist, but Slocum hardly noticed. The huge red spot expanding on the man's back told the story. Edwin had reared up just as lead tore through his shack wall, catching him in the back.

"Not good," Slocum said. "Help me roll him onto his side."

"His side?"

"Put pressure over the wound to keep the hole closed up. I think they got him through the lung. If air gets in, his lung will collapse, and he'll be a goner." Slocum didn't add that he suspected the miner was already a goner, even with all the aid they could give him. "He a chewer?"

"Tobacco? I should say not!"

"Too bad. I need the tinfoil. Is there anything like that? If there is, press it down hard over the wounds—both entry and exit—then tie it into place with a bandage."

"What are you going to do?"

"I've got some hunting to do," Slocum said.

Tabitha grabbed his arm. "You have to tell me. Is Edwin going to live?"

"The bullet went through him. That's good. Having to dig around inside with a knife usually kills more men than it saves. But I don't know if he's a fighter." Slocum saw the concern on the half-naked woman's face. "His love for you might turn the tide," Slocum said with conviction. Then he pulled free and opened the door, only to flop on his belly as a new hail of bullets ripped through where a standing man would have been.

"Who are these sons of bitches?" Slocum called to Tabitha.

"I don't know. I just got here, too."

Slocum smiled grimly. This was close to being gallows humor. He opened and closed the door a few times to draw more fire. He cared less about the flying splinters than he did about emptying the owlhoot's six-shooter. Trying to keep track of how many shots had been fired and from what direction was a fool's errand. When he thought the last slug was fired, Slocum got his feet under him and charged.

He fired as he ran and flushed the outlaw. Rather than waste more lead, Slocum dived and brought the man down in a clumsy tackle. The gunman tried to kick Slocum in the face but only ended up with his leg trapped in Slocum's arms. Slocum had wrestled more than one dogie to the ground in his day. He flipped the man over onto his belly and dropped. He heard a knee break. For an instant there was utter silence, then the outlaw gave out with a cater-wauling that could be heard all the way to Denver.

"Want me to do that to your other leg?"

"No, no, God, I never felt such pain."

"Why were you shooting up the cabin?"

"Gold," the man said. "We figgered to kill the miner and jump his claim."

"That's about equal to stealing a man's horse," Slocum said.

"My leg, oh, damn, it hurts."

"Want me to fix it for you?"

"Do it, do it."

"I'll do it just like I would if my horse busted his leg." Slocum drew his six-gun and fired once. The man stopped screaming. Slocum felt only cold rage at an outlaw who would blindly fire into a shack to kill a mine owner. That it had been when Edwin was getting to know the woman he was going to marry put Slocum in a choleric mood. He had never much taken to Tabitha, but what this outlaw had done shouldn't have ever happened.

A new sound came that put Slocum on guard. It took him a few seconds to recognize the sound of a scattergun action closing.

He headed back to the shack in time to hear the shotgun roar out its throaty death song. Then there was a flurry of cloth and silence.

Slocum ducked back into the shack and looked around. Edwin lay on the dirt floor. A quick check showed that Tabitha had tied two twenty-dollar gold pieces over the bullet holes. Slocum shook his head. He would never have thought of that, but Tabitha had. And it was working. Edwin was pale, but his eyes were open and focused.

"She went after them. Get her, Slocum. Get her. Don't let her die."

"She's a hotheaded woman," Slocum said. "Was that your shotgun she took?"

"Not enough shells for it. Only a few left. Use it for birds."

"Christ Almighty," Slocum said, staring at the wounded man. "You mean she's firing bird shot?"

All he got in way of response was a weak nod. Slocum grabbed a dipper and filled it with water. He put it to Edwin's lips and let the man drink a little.

"Keep sucking on that. Don't move around any more than you have to and you'll be all right. Tabitha's stopped the bleeding." Slocum had no idea what damage had been done inside the man. There was no pink froth on Edwin's lips, so he might have avoided a punctured lung. Even so, he was in bad shape.

"Love her," Edwin croaked out. "I love her. Don't let her die."

"You rest up. We'll be back before you know it."

Slocum took time to reload again, then slipped from the shack and found Tabitha's tracks in the snow. She might not know she was shooting bird shot, which was seldom deadly to a human unless the shotgun bore was pressed right up to the face. Tabitha might not even know there was a difference between hunting for birds and hunting for buck. To her, one shell might be the same as another.

Slocum knew she faced at least one wounded gunman. There might be more—unharmed. As he made his way along her trail, he veered in the direction of a stand of aspens. Something dark smeared the trunk of the white-barked tree. At the base, arms around the trunk, was a dead man. This had to be the one Slocum had plugged during the first minutes of the gunfight. He sucked in his breath, then let it out slowly. White plumes danced on the faint wind stirring through the forest. Tabitha was after another outlaw. An unwounded one.

Finding the trail again was easy, but Slocum found himself going slower and slower as the tracks wended through the forest. It was darker than the inside of a grizzly bear's belly under the tree branches. At times he was almost reduced to going to all fours and feeling for the footprints in the snow. The feeling of impending doom weighed more and more heavily on him, but Slocum refused to hurry. To lose the trail now and have to search for it anew meant Tabitha would end up dead. Her only hope was for Slocum to stay on the trail and finish the man she so inexpertly hunted.

Slocum heard laughter from ahead. He froze, wondering what it meant. Had the outlaw already caught Tabitha and was having his way with her, or did he lure her into a trap? If that was the case, Slocum would be a damn fool to blunder into it, also. He clutched his six-gun and pushed through the undergrowth as silently as he could.

"Go on, little lady. Shoot me. Go on, go on!"

Slocum saw a shadow dart from behind one tree and disappear around another. He slowly changed his position and saw another shadow. This one wore a white blouse and carried a shotgun.

"Come out and fight. You're so big, shooting people from ambush."

"Hell, missy, I'll shoot 'em any way I can. I prefer to shoot 'em in the back. They's not as likely to shoot back!" More laughter. Slocum knew the outlaw was taunting Tabitha to get a response, but the words carried a ring of truth. Claim jumpers were more inclined to gun down their victims when no one was looking—including their victim. It was the lowest of the low when it came to thievery. Slocum was not above a little robbery himself. Banks. Stagecoaches. Cavalry payrolls. But he had never jumped a claim, nor had he shot a man in the back.

Slocum winced when Tabitha fired her weapon. He heard the action opening as she ejected two spent shells and thrust in new ones. By now the outlaw had figured out she was shooting only bird shot and knew it might sting like fire but wouldn't be deadly if he got hit.

"Here. Is this better? You got a good shot at me. Go on. You have the nerve, missy?"

The outlaw stepped out from behind a tree, arms held out at shoulder height to show he wasn't aiming at her. But Slocum saw the pistol in the outlaw's left hand. As the owl-hoot turned, Slocum saw that the man was left-handed.

"You might have killed Edwin!" Tabitha lifted her shotgun and fired both barrels. The recoil staggered her, but she kept her feet.

"That's all you git, missy. Now it's my turn to show you my gun." He reached down with his right hand to unbutton his fly as he pointed his pistol at her.

That was when Slocum braced his hand against a tree trunk, took careful aim, and fired. He had a clear shot and seldom missed. The bullet caught the man in the head. The outlaw jerked to one side, half turned, and then sank to the ground as if all the bones in his body had turned to water. Once he hit the ground, he did not move.

Tabitha let out a shriek of pure anguish.

"I killed him!"

Slocum quickly came up behind her and grabbed the shotgun from her trembling hands.

"I killed him, not you. You wouldn't have even hurt him with bird shot."

"What?" Tabitha looked at him with anguished eyes. "I wanted to, John. I wanted to kill that low-down—" She began sputtering in her confusion and anger.

"You didn't have to. I did it," Slocum said. He had cut down three men in the span of twenty minutes and felt nothing. It was like burning the garbage. These three were worse than anything Tabitha could call them and had gotten their just desserts.

"What's happening, John? I never wanted this. I just

wanted to spend my life with Edwin. He's a good man. He is!"

Tabitha clung to him and cried. He put his arm around her awkwardly and steered her away from the dead outlaw. When her shuddering sobs died down a little, he forced her down onto a stump.

"Wait here a minute. I want to see if I can find out who that son of a bitch was."

Slocum went to the man, took a few paltry dollars in scrip from the man's pocket, then found a folded Wanted poster. Holding it high, he peered at it in the dark. The clouds came and went, but he was treated to enough starlight to see that the likeness on the poster matched that of the dead man.

"A lousy twenty-dollar reward," Slocum said. It was hardly worth claiming. The outlaw had been a petty criminal in all aspects of his thieving life. Slocum crumpled up the poster and tossed it onto the snow by the man's head. Without the body, no lawman would pay the reward. Slocum was not inclined to lug the body through the forest and back into Braden to load into the wagon. The women would not cotton much to riding with a corpse, and Slocum didn't want to deal with the flies and buzzards trying to dine off the bounty. Even if they reached Aurum with the corpse, he wasn't sure where he would find anyone who could pay the reward.

He returned to where Tabitha fought to regain control of her emotions. Bright tears glistened on her cheeks as she looked up forlornly at him.

"He won't be bothering you or Edwin again," Slocum said. He hesitated, then asked, "Are there a lot of claim jumpers out here?"

"I don't know," Tabitha said. "Edwin never mentioned any, but we didn't talk much about things like that. There just wasn't time."

"Come on," Slocum said, putting his arm around her and guiding her back toward the shack. The closer they got to the cabin, the more he worried about what they would find when they opened the door.

Tabitha had to be thinking the same thoughts. Her hand trembled as she pushed against the door, now shot to flinders.

"Edwin?" she called timorously.

Slocum heard movement inside and hoped it was not some bold coyote come to have an early breakfast. He pushed Tabitha aside and went in, hand on his six-shooter. He relaxed when he saw that Edwin had gotten off the floor and collapsed onto the cot. The man's eyes fixed on Slocum.

"Can't offer much in the way of hospitality," Edwin said, "but what's mine is yours." A tiny smile crept onto his bloodless lips. "Except for Tabitha, of course."

"Of course," Slocum said. He found himself shoved out of the way as Tabitha rushed to Edwin's side.

"What do I need to do to make you all better?" Tabitha asked.

Slocum did not hear what Edwin said, but it made Tabitha laugh. Whether the man survived or she had to bury him wasn't something Slocum could predict. He hoped everything went well for them.

"John, wait," Tabitha called. She went to where he stood in the doorway. "I really don't know how to help him."

"Keep him warm and in bed, feed him soup, and keep the wound clean and bound up. Other than that, there's not much anyone can do."

"Is there a doctor in Braden?"

"If there is, I'll have him come out."

"Thank you," Tabitha said. She hesitated, looked a bit shy, then kissed him on the cheek. "You are much better than any of us deserved."

Slocum took better than a half hour tracking down his horse. He checked to be sure it had come through the gunfight without any injuries. Finally satisfied the horse was in top condition, Slocum mounted and headed back down the hill for Braden. It would be dawn soon, and he would find out if there was a sawbones in the town. He would send the doctor out, then he could get back onto the trail with the three remaining mail-order brides.

It was a chore Slocum wanted over as quickly as possible.

11

"Do you think he made it, John?" asked Sarah June. She moved a little closer to him on the hard bench seat as the wagon hit a large rock in the road.

"Who? Edwin? Can't say," Slocum replied. It had been two days since they had left Braden, and the weather had been good. Clear, cold, no snowstorms to slow their progress—he could not have asked for more. Even the snow-packed road had been in remarkably good shape. Slocum had come through Douglas Pass more than once when even riding a horse was dangerous. Drop-offs on the side of the road tended to be precipitous fifty-foot and hundred-foot drops. The poorly kept road often collapsed, sending unwary travelers to their deaths. He had seen more than one spot where wagons had gone down and riders had died and left mute testimony to their last minutes on earth. He had not bothered pointing them out to the three women.

"You must know. You've seen wounds like that before," Sarah June pressed.

"There was one ray of hope in all that," Slocum said. "Braden didn't have a doctor."

"Why is that good?"

"Because the town veterinarian had to go. I'd as soon

have a horse doctor working on me than a drunk surgeon."
He had seen too many doctors during the war hack off
arms and legs and move on while the patient bled to death.
He had never seen a vet fail to struggle to save even obviously terminal equine or bovine patients. Moreover, he had
come across only one drunk vet. More often than not,
liquor was only one of a medical doctor's vices.

"That sounds odd."

"Remember it. You're going to Aurum. I doubt there's a
town doctor, but there has to be a veterinarian somewhere
around."

"You think I'm foolish, going to a town like Aurum,
don't you?"

"I don't know what you're running from," Slocum said.

"I might be running to something, John," Sarah June
said. "Something I need to do."

"Selling yourself to a man you've never even met
doesn't strike me as much improvement over what you had
back in Salt Lake City." Slocum felt the woman tense and
move away from him. She gripped the edge of the driver's
seat so hard her knuckles turned white. Sarah June looked
away from him, but he saw the tension in her shoulders and
the set to her jaw. A pulse in her temple throbbed.

"You don't know, John. You don't know." Sarah June
crossed her arms over her chest.

Slocum turned slightly to hear the chattering between
Wilhelmina and Betty in the rear. Betty had stopped lord-
ing it over the others that she had slept with Slocum, and
the three women were again friends. The main topic of
discussion was Tabitha and what her future would be like.
Betty thought Edwin would die, while Wilhelmina and
Sarah June were sure he would live and Tabitha would live
a glorious life of riches and ease, possibly owning a fine
house in Denver or even Boston.

Slocum hoped that was true, even if it made trouble for
him. He touched his coat pocket where the bag of gold dust

rode. When he got to Aurum, he had to find Tabitha's would-be husband and buy him off. That would not go well, but depending on the man's financial condition, the extra gold dust might go a long way toward easing the pain of not having a bought woman in bed next to him on cold winter nights. If the miner had a wildly profitable claim, he would simply forget the matter and find himself another woman. The worst case would be a miner whose claim was moderately successful. He would feel he had been slighted and might have the stones to try to collect more than Slocum had to offer.

Someone would die in that case, and Slocum knew it would not be him.

"How long will it be, John? Before we get to town?"

Slocum glanced over his shoulder. Betty stared at him with her brown eyes wide and innocent. He knew she was anything but innocent, and there was a hint in her words that she wanted to linger long enough to have another all-night session with him. She was still counting coup on the other two, though she was not as outspoken about it now, and Slocum saw that it worked especially well with Sarah June. The woman had been withdrawn and sullen toward Slocum before. Now she was positively icy. Wilhelmina looked perplexed. She caught the undercurrent between Sarah June and Betty, but her English, as good as it was, failed her when it came to cattiness.

"A few miles. That's the slope leading up to Book Plateau," Slocum said, pointing. The road curved this way and that as it made its way up a steep hill. Atop the mesa were any number of mining towns, but the only one that interested him was Aurum. Not only would he be able to let the women go out on their own to find the husbands who had bought them, he could locate Lemuel Sanders and collect the money due him.

The thought of money turned him to something that had not been discussed; the wagon and team were worth something. Back in Salt Lake City, Preen had probably paid close to a hundred dollars for them. But in Aurum, Colorado, the oxen and wagon might go for a considerable bit more. Nothing had been said about what Slocum ought to do with wagon and oxen when his duties were discharged. He might be able to pocket another two hundred dollars, depending on the market.

"Lagniappe," Slocum said softly.

"What's that?" Sarah June glanced over her shoulder. Her blue eyes were still like chips of ice.

"Nothing," Slocum said. He began whistling, which irritated her even more. If she could have left the wagon and kept up by walking, she would have. Somehow, Slocum no longer cared.

They camped at the base of the road leading up onto the plateau and reached Aurum by sundown the next day.

As they drove in, Slocum studied it. He had the feeling he had been there before. In a way, he had—all boomtowns looked the same. He counted nine saloons along the main street and saw several more on side streets. Aurum was prosperous, as such towns went. Gold flowed out of the mines surrounding it and kept a lively trade going. A quick count showed no fewer than three general stores and two restaurants. That kind of wealth meant a steady commerce between Aurum and Grand Junction, although that city was more than fifty miles away. The wagon and team would fetch a mighty fine price, he believed.

Coal oil lamps were being lit, and the saloons started filling with miners hunting for some surcease from their backbreaking work. The pop skull served in these fine drinking emporia undoubtedly dulled the physical pain and offered a false sense of optimism for the next day's hard work.

"Where do we stay?" Sarah June asked. "Can we find our . . . husbands?" There was a catch in her voice that surprised Slocum. She had hardly spoken of the man who had purchased her, but now he heard an excitement. That shouldn't have been unusual. The woman was going to see her betrothed, but it still set Slocum on guard.

"I don't know. I'll be sure you're bedded down for the night. You can do your hunting tomorrow morning."

"I will," Sarah June said. Again Slocum was startled. There was almost a bloodthirstiness to her that was out of line with being married off. Or was it? Slocum had long since given up trying to figure out women.

"Did you say you'd see us bedded down?" He felt a hand on his shoulder. Betty stood behind him, using his broad shoulders to brace herself as the wagon bounced along the uneven main street. What she hinted was agreeable to Slocum, but he still felt it was his duty to avoid dissension among the women.

"Don't know if there's a decent hotel. Might be, since newcomers need a place to stay until they stake their claims."

Betty bent closer and whispered in his ear, "That wasn't what I meant."

Slocum ignored her as he took a corner and headed for the south part of town. He had seen a crudely lettered sign showing the way to the livery stables.

"Sit down and shut up, you poxy whore," hissed Sarah June. "He's not going to—"

"There we are, ladies," Slocum said loudly, cutting off Sarah June's nasty comment to Betty. "Not much but it'll do."

"That's a hotel?" Wilhelmina spoke for the first time. She looked bewildered. Slocum guessed she might only now realize the enormity of what she had done. She had agreed to marry a man she had never met. In its way, this was as much an arranged marriage as the one she left behind in Salt Lake City. The only difference was that she had agreed to this and had probably received a few dollars from Preen to sweeten the deal.

Slocum doubted it was slavery in the strictest sense, but that didn't mean he had to like it. For Betty, Sarah June, or Wilhelmina.

"I need to find the man Tabitha was going to marry. Do any of you know his name?"

The three exchanged a quick look and all of them shook their heads in unison. Slocum let out a tired sigh. His work was close to being done—but he still had some ways to go.

"Find yourselves rooms. In a town like Aurum, your arrival will be known within an hour. I reckon you all know the men's names who have spoken for you."

"We do," Sarah June said. Her eyes shone with a feverish intensity, while both Betty and Wilhelmina looked more sedate. Or scared. Realization of what they had committed themselves to was slowly sinking in.

Slocum thought he might just sit in the hotel lobby and wait for the men to show up. Tabitha's would-be husband would likely be among the suitors. He could negotiate the woman's choice to stay with another man back at Braden. Somehow, Slocum knew that waiting was not a good idea from the way Betty kept looking at him. He had seen women with that look before, when they thought they'd already roped and branded a husband. Slocum was not going to be any part of that, especially when it meant he would have to deal with two disappointed miners.

Explaining why Tabitha was not among the group would be hard enough. It would be impossible to convince any miner worth his salt that Betty had made another choice and that it was John Slocum.

"What are you going to do, John?" Sarah June asked.

"Go poke under some damp rocks and in dark corners," Slocum said. "Get on into the hotel. I'll see that your belongings are brought over in a spell."

"This is it? The end of the trail?" Betty had tears in her eyes.

"We'll likely see each other before I move on in a day or two. I need to find an old friend before I leave."

Betty gave him a quick kiss. To his surprise, both Sarah June and Wilhelmina did, too. Then they went off to register at the hotel, arms linked and seemingly happy at their uncertain fate.

Then Slocum turned the wagon and team toward the livery stable. He dickered with the stable owner a spell, arranged for the women's trunks to be moved to the hotel, and set off to sample the nightlife in Aurum. Talking to himself, he mused. "Well, Lemuel, I might as well start looking in all the saloons for you. That'd be where you would wash up."

As he sauntered down to the main street, he saw that the women's arrival was already a matter of some discussion. As he walked into the first saloon he came to, a miner reached out a grimy paw and grabbed his sleeve.

"Mister, I seen you drivin' in with them wimmen. Are they whores?"

"Sorry, old-timer," Slocum said. "Wives. All accounted for."

"Them's the ones Rafe and the others bought out of Salt Lake? Do tell. They got themselves some fine-lookin' brides." The miner paused, pursed his lips, then asked, "You reckon they might wanna share?"

"I doubt it, but that's up to both the women and their husbands," Slocum said, amused. He thought of Betty wanting to be shared. Or Wilhelmina or Sarah June. They would rip the throats out of any man even hinting at such an arrangement after what they had left in Salt Lake City.

Or would they? It would be different. The shoe would be on the other foot, with each of the women having as many men as she might want. Even as the idea crossed Slocum's mind, he pushed it away. None of them would go for that. There would be no difference between having many husbands and being a whore working in a saloon.

Slocum found it hard to buy himself a drink. Questions flew from all over the saloon about the women and who might be their prospective husbands. Slocum was woozy when he stumbled from the saloon and went to the next.

More questions about the women cropped up, but a stroke of luck kept Slocum from getting so stewed he couldn't stand up.

"I do declare, I never thought you'd be the one causing the ruckus with them women, Slocum. How the hell you been?"

Lemuel Sanders slapped Slocum on the shoulder and pushed aside the eager miners.

"Boys, this here's my good friend and partner, John Slocum. He's come to Aurum to share my good fortune."

"Do tell," Slocum said. They sank into chairs at the side of the saloon, some distance from the pool table, which seemed to be missing a couple balls and had only one cue stick that had to be passed around. None of the miners took notice of this. They were all trying not to stare at Slocum.

"You're quite a celebrity. Mail-order brides, eh? I considered it, but I hadn't struck it rich yet when that flyer began circulating about buying wives from over in Utah."

"So you've struck it rich now?" Slocum sipped at a shot of whiskey. This tarantula juice was smoother than the raw liquor he had been served in the other saloon.

"No, sir, I haven't. *We* have, Slocum. You put up the stake for my prospecting. That means you're entitled to a share."

"Half?"

"Well, it don't work quite like that. I had a partner helping me out at the mine, but since he's one of them what bought himself a bride, he's not gonna be much help. Has his own claim now, anyway. I got one more partner, back in Utah, who gets a share for all the times we been through together."

"So I get a quarter?"

"That's the way I make it, Slocum. It won't make you a rich man but you'll ride away from Aurum with a damn sight more gold in your pocket than you got now."

Slocum touched the bulge where Edwin's pouch rested. He smiled. He knew Lem Sanders well enough to know the man was inclined to boast. His tales all turned into tall tales, but the respect the other miners showed him convinced Slocum that the strike was rich enough for a quarter share to be worth something.

"I don't have the stomach for working a mine, Lem. You know that."

"'Course I do. I'm planning to make you a fair offer and buy you out. There's nobody what can tie you down, Slocum. I knew that the first time I laid eyes on you. But you'll not be tied down in style. I guar-an-damn-tee it."

"Looks like my trip to Aurum is paying off double," Slocum said.

"Yeah," Sanders said, grinning like a fool. "You and them frisky little fillies. You been on the trail long with 'em? Enough to sample what they have to offer?"

"Can't say that about all of them," Slocum said.

"But a couple? Hell, man, from the gossip goin' around town, all of them's real lookers."

"Started with four," Slocum said. "One decided to stay with a miner over in Braden."

"Four, three, what's the difference? Look, you and them, you're mighty tight after being on the trail. How about you introducin' me to them? Or pick one for me. You know what I like. Blondes are real good. Especially saucy ones."

"That'd be up to them. You might talk to the men who put up good money for them to get here," Slocum said. "Money sometimes trumps lust."

"Lust for money might, but not down and dirty carnal lust." Sanders stared at Slocum, then flat out asked, "Fix me up with one. You know. A blonde. There's a blonde in the lot, isn't there?"

"Two," Slocum said. "One's tall and the other's got fire."

"Either of them. Hell, both. I got me somebody on the inside who can fix me up."

"That's up to them," Slocum said. He saw his friend's face cloud over. Then it darkened with mounting anger.

"You're my partner, Slocum. This ain't the way partners act. You can get them to spend some time with me. An hour or two, just to see how they saddle up and ride."

"I was only the driver, not their pimp. Whatever you do, it's between you and the ladies. And their betrothed."

Lemuel Sanders glowered, then slapped Slocum on the back again. "Let's have another drink or two. Might be, 'fore the night's over, you'll change your mind."

Slocum didn't.

12

Slocum coughed and turned, only to fall out of his chair. He hit the floor and landed on all fours. Blinking hard, he focused his eyes on wood. Boards. A beat-up and battered floor in a saloon. It took a few seconds for him to piece it all together. He turned over and sat heavily, looking up.

"Lem? You in any better shape 'n me?"

"He left, mister. Sanders left more'n an hour ago. He said to fix you a pot of coffee to sober you up so you could get to diggin' out at the claim."

Slocum got to his feet and walked unsteadily to the bar. He leaned heavily to keep from falling. His head felt like a rotted melon about ready to split right down the middle.

"What claim's that?" he asked the barkeep.

"The Lucky Lady. That's Sanders's claim. Him and that other son of a bitch."

"His partner. He mentioned another partner. Somebody he came over with from Salt Lake City," Slocum said. Everything was in his head, but it was all broken apart and needed to be put into a clear picture.

"That's the one. Mean cuss, too. But he got enough money to buy himself a woman after he struck it rich on his own claim. One of them mail-order brides you brung to town is all his, damn him."

"Give me the coffee," Slocum said. He swallowed half the cup before he realized how hot it was. It scalded his mouth and throat, but it woke him up and blew away some of the feathers tickling his brain.

"You look like death warmed over," the barkeep said. "Sure I can't sell you some hair of the dog what bit ya?"

Slocum's belly rebelled at the notion of even one more ounce of liquor being poured into it. He shook his head and regretted it. Things had come loose inside and now rattled about.

"Where can I find the men who bought themselves some wives? I got news for one of them."

"That don't sound good," the bartender said. "There was supposed to be four of 'em."

"Only three made it to Aurum," Slocum said. "I need to make it right with the fourth fellow."

"Well, lemme think. There was Rafe and Slim—that's Slim Nestor, not Slim Dukas—and then Sanders's partner, Heywood. I suspect by now all of them's heard the news and will be showin' up to claim their brides."

Slocum squinted at his watch. It was half past seven. By now most of Aurum would be hard at work in the mines. All but the four men who would be sniffing around the hotel, asking after their paid-for wives.

"Thanks," Slocum said. He downed the rest of the coffee and wondered if he wouldn't have been smarter to take the barkeep up on the drink. As he walked out into the wan autumn sunlight, he felt a mite better. His pace quickened when he saw a big crowd in front of the hotel where the women had spent the night.

Two men were fighting, swinging wildly and hardly connecting. If either had, the other would have a been a goner. Their blows were powerful enough to knock over a horse, but they, like Slocum, had been imbibing too much.

Slocum made his way through the crowd and got to the door leading into the hotel lobby.

"Cain't let you in. Nobody's comin' in," the armed clerk said. He stood with a pistol in each hand, wrists crossed in front of him like he was getting ready to be laid out in his coffin. The expression on his face convinced Slocum that the hotel clerk was not enjoying an instant of this notoriety.

Rather than argue, Slocum slipped along the boardwalk and went around back. The side and rear doors had been nailed shut. This didn't slow him as he grabbed a drain pipe and pulled himself up to a second-floor window. He thought he might have to bust it out with the butt of his six-shooter, but when he peered in, he saw Wilhelmina staring out, eyes wide and frightened. She hastily unlocked the window and heaved it open for him. Slocum tumbled down to the hotel room floor.

"Where are the others?" he asked.

"There is so much confusion," Wilhelmina said. "I did not expect it to be like this."

"You're a valuable commodity. I'm surprised somebody's not been killed fighting over you. Or have they?"

Wilhelmina shook her head, eyes even wider with shock now.

"Good," Slocum said. He danced around Wilhelmina and opened the door into the hallway. Loud voices came from downstairs. Slocum recognized Betty's anguished protests. He took the steps down three at a time. Slocum made certain he kept his six-gun out where everyone could see it.

The clerk turned and started to point his six-shooters at Slocum, then froze.

"I'm not here to cause trouble," Slocum said. "I want to avoid it."

"Then get on into the settin' room and do somethin'. They're about ready to come to blows. Or worse."

Slocum pushed aside tattered drapes and went into the

small room. Betty sat in a chair with a huge miner on each side. Each had a hand on one of her shoulders and pushed and shoved the other with their free hands.

"What's going on?" Slocum called loudly enough to be noticed.

Both men turned toward him.

"Who the hell are you?" demanded the one on Betty's right.

"Call me the judge in this matter. Don't say a word, either of you, or I'll plug you." He saw both men start to protest. He cocked his Colt Navy and waited. They settled down. "Tell me what's going on," he said to Betty.

"It's like this, John. Slim here's the man who sent the money for me."

If Betty hadn't pointed to the man on her right, Slocum would never have guessed this was Slim.

"But Rafe, he thinks he can buy me away from Slim."

"Why's that?" Slocum asked.

"I paid good money for a bride and she isn't here. So I want this one."

"You must have made the contract for Tabitha," Slocum said. Rafe's eyebrows arched.

"You know her?"

"I know what happened to her. Come on over here, and I'll explain." Slocum pointed his six-gun directly at Rafe to make him obey. He acted as if leaving his spot at Betty's side somehow made him forfeit all claim to any woman, but he reluctantly obeyed.

"Sit down," Slocum ordered. He shoved the man down into a flimsy chair that groaned under the sudden onslaught of his weight. "Tabitha is still in Braden."

"She's not hurt none, is she?"

"She found herself another fellow," Slocum said, seeing no reason to pussyfoot around the truth. "He's all shot up, and she's caring for him."

"I don't understand," Rafe said. His face was still flushed, and the anger burning in his eyes was like that of a wild beast ready to pounce.

"She's not coming to Aurum, but she doesn't mean to cheat you. Here's your money back, in gold dust. Along with a little more for your trouble."

"I don't want no dust. I want a woman. My woman!"

"It's not going to happen that way, Rafe," Slocum said. He kept his gun pointed at the miner, who looked like a mousetrap ready to snap the head off anyone coming too close. "You got your money back and then some. Get in touch with Preen and see if he can't arrange for another woman to be sent out. I've heard tell he's got some real fine-looking women waiting to come out here and be miners' brides." Slocum was lying through his teeth, but it hardly mattered. Rafe wasn't listening.

"Gimme," Rafe said, snatching the bag of gold dust from Slocum's grip. "Slim, I'll buy that one from you. Here's a whole bag of dust."

"Go to hell, Rafe. I ain't sellin' Betty. She's my girl. After seein' her, I'm more willin' than ever to marry her, if she'll have me."

"This is too confusing. What do I do, John?"

"That's up to you. Might be a good idea to let things settle down for a day or two before you give a decision," Slocum suggested.

"Slim, please. Will you wait?"

"Ma'am, I'd wait a hunnerd years for a woman like you."

"Rafe?"

Slocum kept his six-gun aimed at the angry miner's gut.

"I want her. I'm gonna have her."

"She might decide that way, but until the lady tells you that's the way she wants it, you leave her be. Understand?"

Rafe got out of the chair and shoved past Slocum. He was outside and in the crowd in seconds. The cacophony that went up made Slocum's blood run cold. Rafe was the kind who would whip a mob into a frenzy.

"Get on out, too," Slocum said to Slim. "I'll talk to her."

"You sure are purty," Slim said as he left.

Slocum collapsed into the chair across from Betty and just stared at her. She was white as a ghost, and her hands shook.

"I never thought it would be like this. Those men were fighting over me."

"Tabitha left a mighty dangerous legacy by not coming along," he said. "It's up to you to get it all straightened out."

"Help me, John. Please."

"Where's Sarah June? Wilhelmina let me in through an upstairs window."

"I think Sarah June rode out of town to find her man. She's been gone since sunup."

"Wouldn't be a man named Heywood?"

"I think so. She said something about half a dollar. I didn't understand that."

Slocum shook his head. Nobody understood anything, least of all him. Why was he still sticking his nose into this mess? He had delivered the women. That was all he had been paid to do. Then he looked at how frightened and forlorn Betty was. She deserved better. Sarah June fit into the social scheme of Aurum well. But Wilhelmina also seemed to be confused and not certain she had done the right thing.

Slocum was beginning to hate what Tabitha had done. She had seen what she wanted and had done it, leaving the troubles it caused for Slocum to clean up.

"I've got a friend here in Aurum," Slocum said. "Let me go palaver awhile with him and see what he knows about Rafe and how to smooth his ruffled feathers. As strangers walking in on him, well, we might not know what's got him so upset." Slocum knew damned well what it was, but he had to keep Betty calm.

"You think you can get everybody calmed down, John?"

Slocum nodded and tried to smile. He wasn't sure how successful he was at it. He waited as Betty returned to her room upstairs, then said to the clerk, "You keep a sharp eye out. There's likely to be trouble."

"Ain't got a marshal in town," the clerk told him. "And if it comes down to turnin' them two over to the crowd or gettin' myself kilt . . ." The man's words trailed off, letting Slocum fill in the rest. It was about as he expected. The clerk didn't have a dog in this fight.

Slocum went to the rear of the hotel and pried off the boards the clerk had nailed across the door, then slipped out. He went across the street to the livery and dickered some with the owner to keep the wagon and oxen for a day or two longer. Slocum knew they were valuable. He also knew he might need the wagon and yoke of oxen to get the women out of town. He had never thought to ask if Betty and Wilhelmina could ride. Going on horseback would be quicker, but neither woman was likely going to leave her trunk and belongings behind.

Swinging into the saddle, Slocum started out of town. He came to the edge of Aurum, where four signposts were festooned with crudely lettered signs directing a traveler to any of half a hundred mines.

"The Lucky Lady," Slocum remembered. He found what might be that name on the fourth signpost, a piece of wood nailed down low. Not certain he was on the right path but deciding anywhere was better than being in town right now, he started riding.

An hour later, he dismounted at the mouth of a mine and saw Lemuel Sanders struggling to push an ore cart out.

"Slocum, you found the place. Didn't know if you'd ever sober up 'nuff to come out, but then you had to see if I was joshin' about the gold. Wasn't that it?"

"Came out to see how your partner's doing with Sarah June."

"You her keeper?" Sanders wiped sweat from his face and left long black streaks. "Or maybe you and her got somethin' going?"

"I need some advice. About Rafe," Slocum said, searching his memory for the name given him by the barkeep. He couldn't remember hearing a last name. "His woman run off with another man, but I paid him what he'd already spent and then some, all in gold dust."

"What are you asking, Slocum? If Rafe's the kind of man to respect a deal like that?" Sanders shook his head sadly. "Nobody crosses Rafe Tornquist. The man's always a fuse burning down to a powder keg. Now and then the fuse is too short and things explode. He's killed a couple men, but nobody in town's willing to face up to him over it."

"No marshal," Slocum said. "When does that stop a bunch of miners from forming a vigilance committee and doing the right thing?"

"Lookee here," Sanders said, taking a rock the size of his fist out of the ore cart and tossing it to Slocum. "That's exactly what you think it is. A vein of gold thicker than a knife blade. I'm assaying out at forty ounces to the ton. This is a big find. Most of 'em on this hill have found gold, too. That's why Heywood lit out on his own, thinking to find a claim matching the Lucky Lady. He found a decent vein. Not as much, not as easy to pry out of the mountainside, but enough."

"Nobody's risking his own neck by crossing Tornquist because everybody's getting rich. Is that it?" Slocum wanted to deal with one problem at a time. Sharing the Lucky Lady's output with Heywood was at the bottom of his problems right now.

"In a nutshell," Sanders agreed. "I told Heywood it was a mistake ordering women like he would a sack of flour, but it's worked out for him. Might be for the best since his temper's worse than Rafe's."

"If I remember rightly, yours isn't the most pacific, either. Thanks," Slocum said. "I know what has to be done."

"Don't get yourself killed, John," Sanders said earnestly.

"I can take twice as much ore out of the Lucky Lady with you helping. You can't do it if you get yourself killed."

"Haven't yet," Slocum said, climbing into the saddle.

"And Slocum," Sanders called, "a word of advice. Don't turn your back on Tornquist."

Slocum rode back to town, considering what had to be done. Betty would be all right if she could settle down with Slim Nestor. All it took for that to happen was some persuading of Rafe Tornquist. Once Tornquist was convinced to leave them alone, Slocum knew the rest of Aurum would do the same.

As he rode to the hotel, he heard the change in the way the crowd was acting. There had been a frantic quality to it before. Each man had wanted to see a woman, if not marry her. Now there was a constant murmuring that set Slocum's nerves on edge. Something was very wrong.

He dropped to the ground behind the hotel and slipped back inside through the door he had unbarred earlier. Long strides took him to the lobby, where the clerk stood with his twin pistols thrust into his belt. In the sitting room, Wilhelmina sobbed softly.

"What's wrong?" Slocum looked from Wilhelmina to the clerk, wondering who would tell him. To his surprise, Wilhelmina spoke up.

"He's dead, Mr. Slocum. Shot in the back."

"Who's dead?"

"The man Betty was to marry."

"Where is she?" Slocum felt as if he had stepped off a cliff and was plunging downward faster and faster.

"After Mr. Slim Nestor was found dead, she was nowhere to be seen," Wilhelmina said.

"Where's Rafe Tornquist?"

"He's more'n likely who backshot Slim," said the clerk from across the lobby. "Don't rightly know, but if I was a bettin' man I'd lay odds that he took the woman, too."

"Where?" Slocum said, a coldness washing over him. "Where would he take her?"

"To his claim, most likely. The Dead Man's Revenge on the other side of yonder hill." The clerk pointed out the front door toward the hill towering about Aurum. "Been workin' a claim there for nigh on two months."

"Alone? Or does he have partners?"

"Has partners. Three of them. All mean polecats, too."

Slocum sucked in his breath, then let it slip slowly from his lungs. If Rafe Tornquist had killed his rival and taken Betty to his claim, there was going to be a slaughter.

Slocum stopped at the general store to buy more ammunition for his Colt and two spare boxes of cartridges for his Winchester. If he was riding into another Antietam, he intended to keep up his end.

To the end.

13

Slocum lay atop a rocky knoll, his field glasses trained on Rafe Tornquist's mine. Sure as rain, the clerk had been right about Tornquist having three partners. The four of them worked the mine together. Even if this wasn't as rich as the Lucky Lady, they took out enough gold to make a good living.

Slocum began to get the feeling that Tabitha had been right for staying with Edwin, no matter if the man eventually died. Coming here, she would have been shared by all four of the men. That sharing could have been one reason Tornquist was so angry when he had not been able to return with a bride. His partners might well have killed him, and he was not going to abandon a quarter of a profitable claim by hightailing it from Aurum to avoid their wrath.

The large cabin some distance away from the mine and its tailings had to be where they kept Betty. Slocum had not seen hide nor hair of the woman, but the miners would not be working so happily if she had escaped.

From the way they toiled, Slocum wondered if they hadn't made some sort of bet that the one who brought out the most pay dirt got Betty first. It was the kind of thing he expected from a man like Rafe Tornquist.

The sun went down fast in the mountains, and at this time of year it got dark by five in the afternoon. That didn't leave Slocum much time. He considered how difficult it would be from his vantage point to simply shoot the four men. During the war he had been one of the best snipers the Confederacy had. But most of his work had been a single shot, a single kill. When Tornquist was in the mine, only one or two of his partners were outside. And when Tornquist came out, they reversed position. The best Slocum could hope for would be to kill a pair of them before alerting the other two.

They might not be mental giants, but they would certainly figure out that whoever was knocking them off like crows on a fence had to be after the woman. Betty's life would be forfeit if even one of the miners reached the cabin. At this range, with only a carbine, Slocum could not count on a clean first kill, much less four.

Waiting until total darkness put Betty into a world of woe. Slocum came to a decision. Boldness had often served him well. It had to now, or more than Betty's honor would be on the line.

He slid back and stood only when he would not be outlined against the sky. He mounted and rode around the far side of the knoll, coming out in a ravine below the cabin, where none of the miners could see him. Riding to the cabin was out of the question. He instead had to climb up a steep slope covered with shale and loose rock.

Slocum worried that he had made a possibly fatal mistake in not bringing a second horse for Betty. The pair of them riding away would tire his horse quickly. He had not seen the corral where Tornquist kept his mounts, but if all four had horses, they would eventually run Slocum and Betty to ground.

Slocum pushed that from his mind. He had a bigger hurdle to clear before any of that mattered. The rocky slope proved even more treacherous than he had anticipated. It took him almost a half hour to reach the top. His hands and knees were cut on the sharp rocks, and he had left a trail of blood even a greenhorn could follow. He flexed his hand, wiped the blood from his palm onto his jeans, and then drew his six-shooter.

Creeping to the cabin, he made a quick circuit to be certain that Tornquist had only three partners. A fourth would be his undoing if he was mistaken. Seeing no trace of a fifth man confirmed what Slocum had guessed about the miners: they did not trust one another sufficiently to leave one as guard while the others worked.

Slocum lifted the latch slowly and pushed open the door. The dim interior was lit by a single sputtering coal oil lamp in the corner. A Franklin stove stood in the center of the room, but from the dank chill inside, the lamp had not been lit recently. A quick move took Slocum into the cabin. He clutched his six-gun firmly and waited for his eyes to adjust.

He heard soft sobbing before he saw Betty all trussed up on a bed at the rear of the cabin. With a quick move, he slid his Colt back into his holster and drew his knife. Slocum crossed the room and knelt beside Betty. The brunette was turned so she faced the back wall. Her hands had been so brutally lashed together they were puffy and white. Slocum put one hand on her shoulder.

She let out a muffled gasp and tried to kick out.

"Quiet," he said. "I'm getting you out of here."

He saw that they had gagged her, too. With a single quick move, he cut the ropes around her wrists. It took him a few more seconds to free her feet. They had bound her securely to keep her from getting away. Only then did he work on the gag in her mouth. Her fingers were too numb to do it herself.

"Oh, John," she sobbed. She threw her arms around his neck and buried her face in his shoulder. He felt his shirt turning wet from her tears. "I thought I was a goner. I tried to kill myself, and they did this to me."

"They'll do a hell of a lot more unless we get out of here," Slocum said. He helped her from the bed, then took a couple logs from beside the stove and covered them with a blanket. It looked nothing like a woman all trussed up on the bed, but if they only glanced in, it might fool them. Slocum needed all the head start he could get.

He helped Betty to the door and looked out. Tornquist and his partners were still working in the mine.

"Kill them, John. Kill them all. Like you did those two mountain men."

"I've got the ammo," he said, "but it's too risky. Believe me, I've considered how I would do it. Getting away is more important."

"They said they're rich," Betty muttered. "But they all wanted me. They were going to take turns. They had a calendar all drawn up showing which day which of them would get to—get to—"

"Come on," Slocum said, steering her out of the cabin. They reached the steep slope. She balked at the stretch ahead.

"No, John, I can't!"

Slocum gave her no choice. He wrapped his arms around her and then simply sat down. After a few feet, he was flat on his back, sliding out of control. He gasped at the pain from all the sharp rocks cutting at his flesh, but he protected Betty enough so that she didn't end up cut to ribbons by the time they tumbled out into the ravine.

"Are you all right, John? My God, your back!"

He winced as he tried to brush the stones away. Most of them were embedded in his flesh. His coat and vest were shredded but had taken the worst of the damage.

"Pull out what you can," he said between gritted teeth. "Then we have to ride. Do it!"

He almost passed out as Betty began plucking the stones from his back, his butt, and his legs. Then he noticed that she had stopped. It took him a few seconds to realize she had finished.

"Are you all right? You look so pale, John."

"Time to ride." He swung into the saddle, then reached down and drew her up behind him. "Sorry if I'm getting blood on you."

"I can't thank you enough for rescuing me." Betty sniffed and held back tears, then added, "Again. Why am I the one who gets into such pickles?"

"Practice?" he joked.

He wheeled his horse around to follow the ravine. As he rode, he worried about where they might be the safest. In town he could recruit some—a few—of the other miners to help protect Betty. But out in the mountains, they could hide. He thought he was more than a match for Rafe Tornquist when it came to such skills. After riding a few minutes, he knew what the answer had to be.

He was too weak to make it back to Aurum.

Eyes blurred from weakness, he looked around and finally spotted a cave high up on the hill, away from the ravine. He got his horse on a dusty track leading to it.

"We can't stop, John. You said it yourself. He'll come after us, madder than a wet hen. If he catches me, he'll . . ."

"I know what he'll do," Slocum said wearily. "And I know what I'll do if I try riding another minute. I need to rest."

"Like before," Betty said. A dreamy quality came over her. "Do you think he can find us?"

"I didn't do much to hide our tracks, but the ground's so rocky he might not be able to figure where we went. I can take a sage bush and erase our tracks."

"I can do that. You need to rest. Like before."

"Like before," Slocum said, so woozy he could hardly stay in the saddle. He knew Betty had dismounted. He almost fell from the saddle. He got his feet under him and led his horse into the cave. It would be another cold night, but there was no hint of snow. That would make it easier going in the morning. Already it was getting dark. Very dark.

Slocum passed out.

Slocum stirred and felt something warm moving next to him. He murmured, then pushed back and sat up. His head spun about for a moment and he feared he had gone blind. Then he saw the dim outline of the cave mouth and a faint pink against clouds, showing dawn was on its way. Looking up at him was Betty. She smiled and pushed her brown hair back from her face.

"Good morning, John. You saved me again."

"Getting to be a habit," he said. "At least it wasn't a pair of nasty mountain men."

"It was a quartet of nasty miners," she said. She reached up and pressed her fingers into his chest. Betty smiled even more. "You have such a strong heartbeat."

"I'm lucky it's still going. Seeing that I had to face four of them to get you away liked to scare me to death."

"I don't believe that. Nothing frightens you."

Slocum hesitated, then said, "You do."

"Do I? What's the scariest about me? The way you enjoy it when I do this?" Betty's fingers moved down his chest and began unfastening the buttons of his jeans. The one at the waist popped open and the fly buttons quickly followed. She fumbled inside his pants and found what she wanted. It was already hot and hard and getting longer by the instant.

The brunette said nothing as she scooted around and moved her face to his crotch. Her lips parted as she took the tip of his erection into her mouth. Slocum shivered as waves of desire passed down his length and exploded in his balls. There was no way he could get any harder. Her mouth moved over the thick, bulbous tip of his cock and then took more into her mouth. And more and more until he thought she would swallow him whole. He felt the rubbery head of his manhood bounce off the roof of her sucking mouth and then work deeper into her throat.

He closed his eyes and shivered again. Desire built within him until he wanted to cut loose and let his hips drive his fleshy spike forward. But he held himself back to enjoy the moistness, the warmth, the way her tongue worked over the most sensitive parts, hidden away in her mouth.

"Umm," she said, working her way back so she could look up at him. "You're tasty."

"And you want more than that in your mouth, don't you?"

"You know what I want, John. I want this," she said, gripping his steely spike and pulling downward. "And I want it here." Betty hiked her skirts and rocked back on the cold stone floor. Her knees came up and then parted, wantonly revealing her privates.

Slocum let her guide him around, but he was the one who positioned himself at just the right point for the proper insertion. He felt the heat boiling from her innards. Then he experienced it fully. He sank deep into her molten center. He gasped when she squeezed down on him, her velvet sheath tightening. Moist, hot, tight—he was in heaven.

"Move, John, move. Give it to me. Give it all to me hard!"

He began pulling free. He reared up and braced himself on her raised knees, looking down into her lovely face. Her eyes were closed, and the expression on her face showed the level of her arousal.

Slocum shoved back in. The friction of his cock against her inner walls built as he started stroking with deep, sure strokes. He felt her nether lips engorge with blood and stroke along the sides of his erection every time he moved. So he moved faster to get more of this subtle, delightful stimulation.

Soon they were striving together, moving hips in unison to garner the greatest stimulation possible. Slocum panted harshly and fought to hold back the urge to let himself rush free.

"Yes, John, do it now, do it, please, ohhh!"

The sound of Betty's emotional and physical release worked on him. She tensed powerfully around his hidden cock and then he could no longer control himself. His volcanic come spewed forth and all too soon he began to melt within her. Slocum sank forward, pressing her down to the rock floor. Faces only inches apart, he waited for Betty to open her eyes. Then he kissed her.

"You're special, John. How I wish you—"

"What?"

"Nothing, nothing," she said, beginning to writhe about under him in a manner showing she wanted his weight removed. He rolled to the side. Betty turned, looked down at his flaccid organ, then gently tucked him away. She sat up and pulled down her skirt where it had bunched around her waist. Once more she looked almost prim.

Almost.

"We need to get away from here, or Rafe will come after me," she said.

"He'll be hard-pressed to find our trail."

"There were only two ways we could have gone from where we slid down the side of the mountain," she said. "Even Rafe could figure out we had to go one way or the other."

"He's a lazy son of a bitch," Slocum said. "And a coward. He shoots men in the back to save himself the effort of getting into a real fight."

"That makes him all the more dangerous. And there are four of them. They could split up and two could go each way along the ravine. They can find us. Rafe will want to find me almost as much as the others will."

"A matter of pride," Slocum agreed. "More than that, he shot a man in the back to kidnap you. He would take it as an insult that he lost you after going to that much trouble."

"Slim's dead?"

"Very," Slocum said. He considered for a moment and realized she would not have known. Rafe might have bragged on killing Slim Nestor, but more likely he was too intent on sampling the feminine delights Betty offered.

"Please, I want to get back to town."

"What then?" Slocum asked. He had worked the problem over in his head and saw no easy solution. If Betty stayed in Aurum, Rafe would keep coming after her and more men would die. The only way out looked to be her leaving.

It was a good thing he had not sold the wagon and team. The thorn in his side, though, was wondering if he wanted Betty riding along with him. She had the look of a woman wanting to put a brand on his hindquarters. Slocum wasn't ready to be corralled by any woman, but that was the way she would see it if he let her come with him when he left Aurum.

"Can't rightly say," she answered. "Something will come to me." She looked at him and batted her eyelashes. That told him his guess was right. She was thinking of him as her exclusive property.

Slocum got to his feet and went to the cave mouth. He stared out into the dawn. Deeper in the cave, his horse nickered. Getting the horse to water and letting it graze awhile was necessary if he wanted it to carry both his and Betty's weight all the way back to town. He stepped out, stretched, and knew something was wrong. Very wrong.

He threw himself to the side an instant before a bullet whined past him and ricocheted off a rock. Slocum grabbed for his six-shooter, but found he had not bothered to put it on before coming out to get the lay of the land.

Slocum kept rolling and came up behind a boulder so he could see the hillside above the cave mouth. The glint of morning sunlight off the barrel of a pistol told the story.

"Didn't think you would find me, Rafe," Slocum called. "But now that you have, it makes sense you'd try to shoot me in the back. Like you did Slim Nestor. Like you probably have done a dozen times before."

"Not that many, but you'll be one closer to that dozen, Slocum."

"She doesn't want you or your partners, Rafe," Slocum said. "Let her go."

"I paid for a woman, and I'm gonna take *her*!"

He fired a couple more times, but the shots were made in anger. He missed by a yard, though it drove Slocum down behind the rock. If Tornquist ever figured out he didn't have a six-gun, the miner would come rushing down the hill to finish the job he had started.

Slocum peered around the rock and saw a frightened Betty standing just inside the cave mouth. He made silent gestures showing the danger. Betty nodded numbly. Then Slocum made shooting motions and pointed to his bare hip. He repeated the shooting gesture.

Betty disappeared into the cave.

"You ain't firin' at me, Slocum. That mean you're outta ammo? Or maybe you don't have your smoke wagon. That it?" Rafe Tornquist stood, fully exposing himself. When no bullet ripped at him, he laughed heartily. "You ain't got a gun! That's rich."

Tornquist slipped and slid down the slope, heading directly for Slocum.

"You're fixin' to meet yer maker, Slocum. I want to kill you real slow so you don't fergit Rafe Tornquist fer the rest of eternity you spend in hell!"

"I won't forget you, Rafe," Slocum said, moving from behind the rock. Betty threw him his Colt Navy from just inside the cave. Slocum went into a gunfighter's crouch as he grabbed the six-shooter in midair and began fanning the hammer. All six bullets struck Rafe Tornquist in the chest. The miner took a few more steps, lifted his pistol, and stared at it stupidly. His eyes rose to Slocum, then he fell facedown and slid past in the loose gravel.

Slocum watched as the miner came to a halt a yard beyond. He looked up at Betty where she stood with a hand over her mouth.

"Let's ride," Slocum said. "It's time we got back to town."

14

"What do you think the other three will do?" Betty asked.

"Hard to say. I doubt there's a whole lot of friendship among them. If anything, they would see Tornquist's death as giving them a bigger slice of the pie."

"The mine's got a lot of gold in it," Betty said. "I heard them talking. They got more than enough to send for me."

"For Tabitha," Slocum corrected.

"Yes, of course, for Tabitha. But when she never arrived, they claimed they had paid for me."

Slocum wondered what Rafe had done with the bag of gold dust that Edwin had sent to settle accounts. It was a minor point, but Slocum still wondered if he might be able to retrieve it. He wanted something for all his trouble. He felt the pretty woman's arms around his waist and smiled a little. He wanted something more as a reward than what he had already received for rescuing Betty. All he had been paid to do was deliver the women. Nothing had been said about guarding them once they had arrived in Aurum.

"Would what happened back there be considered a common-law marriage?"

"What?" The question took Slocum by surprise. "I don't follow you."

"Well, I was in Rafe's bed and he claimed me. Does that mean we were married?"

"Reckon the lawyers would have fun with that," Slocum allowed. "There might be the question of consummating the marriage. With you all bound up and gagged, there wasn't much chance of that."

"Oh, really?"

Slocum glanced over his shoulder. "You mean the son of a bitch raped you while you were all trussed up like a Christmas goose?"

"Could have," Betty said coyly. "You couldn't tell, could you? It's just my word against that of a dead man."

"And his partners."

"They weren't there all the time. I was alone with Rafe."

Slocum wondered what Betty was angling for. He frowned as he considered all she was saying. Betty had not mentioned Rafe taking advantage of her once she had been tied up. From what he could tell from his brief observation from the knoll across from the mine, the four were waiting to take turns. Rafe Tornquist might have started early, but Slocum thought Betty would have mentioned it before now. She had been incensed at the miner, but in her words there had not been the outrage of a raped woman.

"There's the edge of town," Betty said. "Is there a judge in town?"

"There's not even a marshal," Slocum pointed out. "A circuit judge comes through once in a blue moon. Otherwise, Aurum is wide open."

"There must be a mayor," Betty pressed.

"Never heard. Closest thing to law in a boomtown like this would be the land agent. He usually doubles as assayist as well as county recorder. Might even try to collect tax, though I doubt he's too successful. Any real law enforcement would be done by a vigilance committee."

"A land office," Betty mused. "Let me get off at the land

office, John. I need to ask some questions about the Dead Man's Revenge."

She dropped to the muddy street and looked up at Slocum. Her brown eyes positively glowed. Betty smiled and touched his arm, then swung about, skirts swirling, and rushed into the land office. Slocum rode a few yards, then curiosity got the better of him. He dismounted and sauntered back to the land office. The door stood open, and he could see Betty and the land agent behind the counter. The man wore wire-rimmed glasses, had sandy, thinning hair, and looked to be about forty. He was lapping up all the attention Betty lavished on him.

"That doesn't seem fair, not at all, Mr. Fremont."

"Call me Franklin," the land agent said, pushing his eyeglasses up with his index finger so he could get a better look at his lovely client.

"Why, thank you, Franklin. And you must call me Betty. Now, tell me it isn't silly for a man's wife not to inherit his claim."

Slocum straightened and turned so he could lean against the wall of the land office and listen to what went on inside without drawing attention.

"That's the way it is. Ever since Colorado became a state, there've been all kinds of absurd laws."

"But not one preventing a widow from benefiting from her husband's hard work."

"You and Rafe, you are married?" Franklin Fremont sounded uneasy.

"Were, Franklin, were. We *were* married. Rafe met an untimely end. The frontier can be so cruel."

"And it can be kind," the man said. "Please, Betty, come on around and set yourself down. Tell me all about it."

"Oh, Franklin, you're so kind. It was tragic. His partners turned on him and shot him down. All three of them. Each put a couple slugs into poor Rafe and left him some distance from the mine."

"The Dead Man's Revenge mine," Franklin said sympathetically.

"That was so aptly named. Ironic, too," Betty said, sniffing slightly

"So you and him was hitched."

"Common-law marriage," Betty said.

"Then you might be able to claim some part. Now, proving Rafe's partners had anything to do with his killing might be hard."

"How could I possibly accept those three as partners, knowing they are stone killers?"

"Might be a town meeting could put a fear of God into them. Been a while since we whupped up a committee of vigilance to set things right."

"Oh, Franklin, is that possible? But they would flee! They know they are guilty. They would not want to be brought to justice for killing my husband."

Slocum had heard enough to know how Betty maneuvered the land agent to see things her way. A town meeting might produce the vigilance committee, but it would be going after the wrong men. Still, Slocum appreciated how easily he had been extricated from the problem. He smiled ruefully. Betty's story did more than exonerate him. It made it impossible for anyone but Betty to make any claim on the mine without sticking his own neck into a noose.

Running Rafe's three partners out of the state would improve life in Aurum, but Slocum felt uneasy at the way Betty was doing it with her easy lies. He walked away, shaking his head. He had to admire her for her daring. She had turned a terrible experience into one that might make her rich. If Betty had not come up with this scheme, he suspected she would have worked some other confidence game. He had seen this in her and had denied it to himself.

Slocum started back to the hotel to see how Wilhelmina

was faring. He heaved a sigh of resignation when he saw the huge crowd still milling about.

Loud voices came from the direction of the hotel, but they were not arguing. As he approached, he tried to get a better view, but too many miners blocked him from seeing the hotel porch.

"What's going on?" Slocum asked.

"Auction."

"What's being . . ." Slocum's voice trailed off as he heard the stentorian voice of the hotel clerk call, "Mr. Elkhardt is willing to give up his right to this fine young lady in exchange for one hundred dollars, gold."

"He's auctioning off his mail-order bride?" Slocum stared in wonder. Then anger built. Wilhelmina was not chattel. He pushed through the crowd until he was at the front, but he hesitated when he saw how Wilhelmina beamed. The man beside her—Elkhardt—looked excited, but nobody was in the least upset. If anything, there was a carnival atmosphere about this.

"The bidding starts at one hundred dollars," the hotel clerk called. "Anything in excess of this will be split between Miss Wilhelmina and Mr. Elkhardt."

"Two hunnerd!"

"Three!"

Slocum saw the miners searching their pockets for bags of gold dust and even nuggets. Wilhelmina had put herself up for auction after coming to some accommodation with the man who had bought and paid for her.

"Why's he giving up such a good-looking woman?" Slocum asked.

"Money. Elkie's flat broke. His mine petered out, and he heard 'bout a new strike up north, almost at the Wyoming line. With a good stake, he can get rich up there and have his pick of the women in Denver."

"But Wilhelmina is here, and he's already paid for the right to marry her."

"They didn't hit it off so good. Woman's always got the right of refusal, but she's got to repay the man. Them's the rules."

Slocum heard the bidding turn frenzied as miners saw a chance to do more than buy a pig in a poke. Elkhardt had taken a risk that the woman sent over from Salt Lake City would be ugly with the disposition of a rabid skunk. Wilhelmina was none of those things, but the lure of gold was greater than his need for a wife.

Slocum wondered if Elkhardt and Wilhelmina had decided on this auction before or after going to bed. It hardly mattered. Wilhelmina would be wealthy in her own right from her future husband's bidding. And Elkhardt would have more than enough money to outfit him for a season or longer of prospecting.

Slocum drifted away from the crowd when the bidding hit one thousand dollars. Wilhelmina was certainly no pig in a poke now. She was stately, pretty, and willing to go with the man who had the most money.

Both Betty and Wilhelmina had found their way to getting what they wanted most, as had Tabitha. A woman might not be able to own real estate, but she could maneuver around and become rich in her own right.

"John! John!" He turned to see Sarah June waving to him from the front door of a mercantile.

"Howdy, ma'am," he said, tipping his hat to her. She beamed at him.

"It's good to see you, John. I heard about what happened with Betty. How terrible."

"She's making it all good," Slocum said, looking in the direction of the land office. He saw Betty arm in arm with the land agent as they left.

"I'm happy for her. What about you? Are you all right?"

"Fine as frog's fur," he said. "You pleased with your husband?" He saw the fever burning in her eyes. As if she worried that he might see, the light faded and she turned partly away from him.

"Oh, yes, I am quite happy. I am sure in the coming days I will be even happier."

"Heard tell Heywood is rich."

"Oh, not at all. That doesn't matter to me. It's the man I wanted most."

Slocum hesitated. Lemuel Sanders had said Heywood was a partner in the Lucky Lady, and Slocum had seen for himself the riches coming from the depths of the mine. He wondered if Heywood was hiding some of the gold from his new wife, though in Aurum that seemed a bit far-fetched. Everyone knew everyone else's business. All Sarah June had to do was ask.

"Glad that you're settling in just fine, Sarah June."

"You'll have to come out to the Sombrero some time and visit, John."

"The Sombrero?" Slocum was puzzled.

"That's his mine. You just ride north of town until you see a signpost. There's a marker telling how to get to the mine."

"Don't rightly know if I'll have a chance," he told Sarah June, "because I want to be on my way. All you ladies have finally gotten settled. There's nothing keeping me here." Slocum wondered what Sanders would give him for his share in the Lucky Lady. It was about time to find out. He bid Sarah June good-bye and saw how she seemed reluctant.

If they had not been in public, he thought she would have kissed him.

Slocum got his horse and left Aurum, riding straight to the Lucky Lady mine. As before, Sanders worked like a fool moving ore from the depths of the mine and dumping it in a glittering pile just at the mouth.

He waved to Slocum, hailing him. "Come on up, Slocum. We got work to do, you and me. This here ore's begging to be separated. Then we can cart it down to the smelter in the valley and get even richer."

Slocum tethered his horse behind the cabin, took off the saddle, and slung his holster over the saddle horn. If he was going to put in a day's work, there was no need to have three pounds of iron at his hip.

"What do you want me to do?"

"You've done it before, I reckon. Sort the dross from the rock with gold in it."

Slocum began working and found enough gold in every hunk of rock to merit smelting. After an hour of work, he had a very small pile of dross and a large one of rock with gold in it.

"Let's take a break," Sanders said. He wiped sweat from his forehead. "Looks like a bad batch from the mine today."

"What do you mean? There's hardly any rock compared with the gold-bearing."

"The Lucky Lady doesn't produce bad rock. This is, well, this mine's a gold mine, Slocum."

Sanders went to the cabin and returned with a bottle. He pulled the cork and took a deep drag.

"That's for what ails you. My muscles don't ache quite so much after a few snorts."

Slocum took a pull himself, then got down to a question he had been working on ever since he had gotten to the mine. "Where's our partner? Where's Heywood?"

"You found out, didn't you? Or did you figure it out on your own?"

"Tell me," Slocum said, not sure what Sanders meant.

"I bought him out right after we got to Aurum. Heywood was never too bright when it came to finding blue dirt. I knew right off the Lucky Lady was my ticket to riches. He thought he could do better."

"At the Sombrero mine."

"I always knew you were sharp, Slocum. It didn't take you hardly any time at all to figure it out. Yeah, that's his mine. Not great, but this whole damn region's rife with gold. Heywood's not getting rich, but he's not starving, either."

"I want to know the entire story, not just pieces," Slocum said. He took a long draw on the whiskey and let it slip down his gullet to warm his belly. He realized it had been a while since he had eaten anything. The fiery liquor made him light-headed even as it gave him new strength to work another few hours.

"Me and you were partners back in Salt Lake City."

"Not so much partners as friends. That's when you got the stake from me," Slocum said. "I felt I owed you."

"You loaned me the money, went your way, and I teamed up with Heywood, Yarrow, and Carson."

"Carson? Yarrow?" Slocum had no idea who these men were.

"The four of us cut quite a swath through Salt Lake City, then Carson cut out on us and went his way. But me, Yarrow, and Heywood came straight out here 'bout six months back."

"That's when you found the Lucky Lady and Heywood went off on his own to work the Sombrero? And Yarrow got a mine of his own, too?"

"Yup," Sanders said, putting the cork back into the bottle. "Wish you coulda shared some of the times the four of us had in Salt Lake. The Silver Dollar Boys, that's what they called us."

Slocum stared at his partner. He had seen Wanted posters for the Silver Dollar Gang offering hefty rewards. Try as he might, he could not remember what crimes had been mentioned, not that it mattered much. Slocum's own past was checkered with Wanted posters for more crimes than he could remember. Killing a carpetbagger judge back in Georgia was the most serious of the crimes, but he was anything but pure as the wind-driven snow.

"The name was Carson's idea. He wanted secret handshakes and passwords and I don't know what all." Sanders laughed. "Me and Heywood always figured it was because

Carson had tried to get into the Masons or Elks and they wouldn't have him, so he started his own secret society. We went along because he knew his way around Salt Lake City and the rest of us didn't."

"So you came here because you had to? One step ahead of the law?"

"Something like that," Sanders admitted. "But you caught me trying to do you out of your share in the Lucky Lady. Or at least cut it down, and for that, John, I offer my apology."

Slocum nodded. If Sanders had made him think he owned only a quarter of the mine, that meant he had to pay less when he bought him out.

"Carson the other partner?"

"I threw him in, just to see if I could get by with it. He's back in Utah. Never came out here. No, John, you and I are half owners of the Lucky Lady. And there's something I want to show you."

Slocum tensed. Sanders wasn't the confessing sort. He wished he had not left his six-shooter hanging around his saddle horn.

"Come on into the mine. Oh, don't worry your head none. I'm not fixing to do you in."

Sanders went into the mine, Slocum following a few feet back. Sanders found a shelf with miner's candles, lit two, and handed one to Slocum.

"I'd dug purty near a hundred yards into the hillside and never noticed this until yesterday. You showing up was a sign. You brought me—us—good luck."

Sanders held a miner's candle above eye level to show a bright gold vein almost an inch thick in the wall.

"If that runs more than a foot or two, we're richer than we ever dreamed of being."

Slocum stared at the mother lode, speechless. He was rich!

15

Slocum came out into the bright autumn sunlight and noted how short the days were becoming. That hardly mattered when he spent most of the day underground, choking on the fumes from candles and swinging a pickax to pry loose the precious gold from the mine walls. He sat on a rock and let the sun warm him. He stared at the small mountain of rock they had pulled from the Lucky Lady in the past week.

Any part of that would make him a wealthy man. If he kept working alongside Lem Sanders, he would be rich enough to buy a fancy mansion in Denver, go to the opera and have his own box, and eat oysters and drink French champagne. The only problem with all that was how much he hated big cities, had no desire to live in a house with more rooms than he could count, had no appreciation for the caterwauling opera, and thought eating oysters was like swallowing snot. Of the things rich people did, drinking champagne was the one that appealed most to him.

Harkening back more years than he really cared to remember, he had captured a wagonload of Gran Monopole champagne destined for some Yankee senators and their wives and mistresses come out to watch a battle. He had scared off the politicians and their ladies and had ten cases of the fine champagne all to himself. He had divvied it up among his men, but he still had gotten royally drunk on four bottles.

He could do that again, and this time he didn't even have to chase off any Yankee senators. He could buy it. He could hire someone to buy it for him.

This was the life.

Slocum wanted to move on. Soon.

He squinted when he saw dust being kicked up on the road below. He had put the wagon and the yoke of oxen to good use. Every other day, either he or Sanders drove a load of ore down into the valley, where the crusher worked overtime sending gravel into the smelter. He had made two trips and Sanders one during the past week, and they had more than a hundred dollars a day to show for their work. Each.

He threw his pick down and brushed dust off his clothing. He was a walking dust devil. Slocum walked down to the spot where they loaded the ore into the wagon.

"What took you so long?" Slocum called to Sanders. "I've got an entire wagonload ready to go. You haven't been lollygagging in town again, have you?"

Slocum saw the expression on Sanders's face and stopped his joshing. Something serious had happened. His friend normally had a hair-trigger temper, but of late, with everything going so well, Lemuel Sanders had been joking and carrying on like a schoolboy. That good humor was gone.

Sanders fixed the reins around the wagon brake and jumped down.

"He's dead, Slocum. Deader than a doornail."

"Who's that?"

"Heywood. An accident over at the Sombrero mine, I heard."

"What happened?" Slocum asked.

"Nobody knows. They haven't recovered his body yet from the mine. You mind coming with me? I want to give the son of a bitch a decent burial, though he hardly deserves one."

"You driving the wagon?"

Sanders nodded glumly. Slocum saddled his horse and trotted along to catch up. Sanders had left immediately, forcing Slocum to hurry.

"You think it might not be an accident?" Slocum knew his partner well enough to see that something troubled him.

"Hell, mining's a dangerous profession. Heywood was not what you'd call a careful man, either." Sanders looked over at Slocum riding alongside the wagon. "You think I have a bad temper. Heywood would fly off the handle at the slightest thing. He might have done something really dumb while he was in the mine. Ax handle breaks, he could have gone berserk and collapsed the mine on his own head. I don't know. He had quite a temper."

They rode the rest of the way to the Sombrero mine in silence, each wrapped in his own thoughts. The death of Sanders's former partner set Slocum to thinking again on moving on. He had taken a fortune out of their mine in the past week. If he asked Sanders to buy him out for a thousand dollars, that would last him for years and yet hardly put a dent in the mine's output. Sanders would get rid of a partner sucking up half the profit, and Slocum would have more money than he had ever dreamed about. And he would be free to drift wherever the wind took him.

As cold as it was getting at night, Slocum considered finding a nice warm señorita down south of the border to keep him company all winter long.

"There's the mine," Sanders said. Slocum wheeled his horse onto the small rutted track leading up to the Sombrero mine. He saw Sarah June sitting in a chair outside a tumbledown shack. She had her head down, and he thought she might be crying, but as he neared he saw she was reading a newspaper. She looked up, smiled when she saw him, carefully folded the paper, and rose to greet him.

"I hadn't expected to see you, John. How good of you to come."

Slocum had expected a grieving widow, but Sarah June looked as if her day included nothing more upsetting than having her newspaper reading interrupted.

"Sorry to hear about your husband," he said, dismounting.

"Tragic," she said. He expected a tear or at least a frown. If anything, she showed her dimples as she smiled at him.

"That there's Lemuel Sanders," Slocum said. "My partner over at the Lucky Lady."

"The Lucky Lady? You're a partner? That's a mighty important mine in these parts."

"Can't complain," Slocum said. He stared at the mine shaft. The timbers were intact. "That where he died?"

"Yes, inside," Sarah June said. She turned and stared at Sanders. The expression on her face was unreadable now. "How good of you to come along with Mr. Slocum."

"Felt it was my duty," Sanders said, tipping his hat to her. "Don't reckon you want to keep the body around. If you don't mind, we'd like to get it on into town for a burial. Unless you have other plans?"

"I sent word into town that the body was, well, difficult to reach."

"In the mine shaft?"

"A deep pit," Sarah June said.

Slocum watched the blonde staring at Lemuel Sanders as if she tried to place him but couldn't.

"Let's go see what can be done," Slocum said. "Are there lanterns in the mine?"

"Two," Sarah June said. "If you don't mind, I would prefer to stay out here. The sun is quite pleasant today."

"Get on back to your newspaper," Sanders said a bit sharply. Slocum understood Lemuel's attitude. He and Heywood had been partners. Slocum had known Sanders for only a short while, but he had the feeling that Sanders had been partnered up for quite a spell. Certainly far longer than the six months they had been in Aurum and whatever time they had spent in Salt Lake City.

Slocum and Sanders trudged uphill to the mine. Slocum kicked at rock all around, hunting for the bright shine of gold in the rocks. He saw some iron pyrite—fool's gold—but nothing worth hauling to the smelter.

"Not a good claim," he said when they ducked and went into the shaft. Just inside, on a rock shelf, they found the two lanterns Sarah June had mentioned. Slocum worked to light them, then sloshed the kerosene around. "Not more than an hour's light in either of them."

"Shouldn't take that long getting a body out," Sanders said.

"He was a good friend, wasn't he?"

Sanders spat. "I went from hating his guts to thinking of him as my brother and back again, sometimes in an hour's span. What it all came down to was how alike we were. I said he had a temper. So do I. Somehow, we shared in ways most folks never can."

"You understood each other."

"Let's just say we took pleasure in the same ways," Sanders said. He held his lantern up high and started into the mine.

Slocum saw that Heywood had not bothered to lay tracks for an ore cart. That meant extra work in the long run, because he had to use a wheelbarrow to get his gold out of the mine. As he walked bent over, Slocum studied the walls, hunting for gold. He saw a few flecks, but nothing like in the Lucky Lady.

"Hold up, Slocum. This must be where Heywood got careless."

Slocum poked his head around Sanders's shoulder and

saw a yawning chasm in the floor. The light from the lantern penetrated only a few feet down. The pit was far deeper than that.

"You reckon he fell in? What's he doing digging a pit like this?"

"No telling what Heywood was up to," Sanders said. "No good, that's my opinion." Sanders moved his lantern around, looking at the edge of the pit. "Don't see that the rock gave way."

"May have been drunk," Slocum said. He kicked a pint bottle out of the way and dropped to his belly so he could look down into the hole. The lantern barely illuminated the bottom. "That must be twenty feet down."

"He could have survived," Sanders said.

"Unless he was drunk when he fell in," Slocum replied.

"That makes it all the more likely he would survive," Sanders said. "He would have been crawling around on the bottom wondering what had happened."

"I see what must be his body." Slocum turned his head to the side. He could see moderately well, but the smell of decay rising from the pit was enough to gag him.

"I'll go fetch him up," Sanders said. "It's the least I can do, since he was my partner."

"Don't know how easy it'll be getting you out," Slocum said. He looked at the beam overhead. "Might be able to rig a pulley. The timber looks safe enough for that." Slocum checked the strength of the beam, then ran his hands down the supporting timbers. He knelt when he saw a section of the wood that had separated.

He frowned when he saw that it was a loose board. Bloodstains on the side gave mute testimony to a serious accident. Heywood must have hit his head and then fallen into the pit.

"Let's do it. The sooner I get Heywood out, the better I'll like it."

They worked in silence for almost twenty minutes, setting a pulley just above the pit and fixing a rope with a loop for Sanders to slip his shoulders through. Once it was around his body, he nodded. Slocum took up the slack, then began lowering. The pulley creaked and the beam protested, but everything held until there was suddenly no weight on the rope.

"You down?"

"Yeah. Rats got to him. How long's he supposed to have been dead?"

"Sarah June never said," Slocum called down. "Must have been a day at the outside, though, or you would have been told earlier."

"From what's left, he might have been here for three or four days."

Slocum felt the rope tighten. He began pulling and brought the body up. His gut flip-flopped when he saw Heywood. Sanders had not been joking about the degree of decay or how the rats had feasted. How they got in and out of the pit Slocum didn't want to know, but he had seen rats run up and down almost vertical ropes.

"He must have been going down into the pit," Slocum said, as he swung the corpse around and laid it out on the floor of the mine. "There's bits of rope he must have used to lower himself." Slocum stood, held the lantern, and stared. Heywood had not used the rope to lower himself. It looked as if the rope had been lashed around his feet.

"Get that rope back down here. This pit's giving me the willies," Sanders shouted.

Slocum quickly pulled it free from around Heywood and dropped the loop back to Sanders. It took longer getting his partner up because the beam began to sag and Slocum worked more carefully. When Sanders set his feet on solid rock, he heaved a deep sigh of relief.

"That's nothing I want to do again until I'm actually planted in a graveyard," he said. "It felt like I was in a grave the whole time."

"Did you tie his feet together to make it easier for me to pull him up?" Slocum asked.

"I just looped it around his waist. Hell, touching him was bad. I seen men blown up in explosions that didn't cause my stomach to churn like it did down there."

Slocum understood. The body was in bad shape. He looked around, found burlap bags, and spent the next half hour fashioning a shroud for Heywood. By then Sanders had fetched the wheelbarrow. They dropped the body in, and Slocum wheeled it out into the bright light of the Colorado afternoon.

"You can get it into the wagon," Slocum said.

"You just want to cozy up to the widow woman," Sanders said. "Don't much blame you. She's real purty." He grabbed the wheelbarrow handles and got the grisly cargo rolling down to the wagon, where the oxen began to nervously move about. They had caught the scent of the body.

"We got him out, Sarah June," Slocum said. The blonde stared at Sanders struggling to lift and load her dead husband into the back of the wagon. Slocum wondered what thoughts ran just behind those bright blue eyes. Her husband being carted off to the cemetery in the same wagon that had brought her and the other women from Salt Lake City? Or was it something more? Slocum could not tell.

"Thank you, John."

"How long ago did he die?"

"Why, a day or two. It was hard for me to determine."

"If he didn't come to dinner, that'd be a sign something was wrong."

"What are you saying?" She turned and looked at him sharply.

"He's been dead for longer than that," Slocum said.

Sarah June just shrugged and looked unconcerned.

"Then there's the matter of how his feet were tied together."

"What do you mean?"

"I'd say his feet were bound before he fell into the pit. Might be the reason he fell into the pit."

"Are you saying that he might have stepped into a lasso, which was yanked tight around his legs, and then he was pushed into the pit? What a vivid imagination you have, John."

Sanders trooped up and took off his hat. "You have my sincere condolences, ma'am. It can't be easy losing a husband."

"I only knew him a short while," Sarah June said. Slocum saw how she looked at Sanders like a hungry coyote stalking a rabbit. "You must have known him ever so much longer."

"Long enough to feel a loss," Sanders said. He jerked his head in the direction of the wagon, then put on his hat and walked briskly downhill to where the oxen were increasingly agitated at their cargo.

"I'll see to the funeral. There's only one funeral parlor in Aurum," Slocum said. "Don't think there'd be any problem getting Heywood buried tomorrow."

"I'll go into town later today," Sarah June said. As Slocum turned to go, she grabbed his arm and stopped him. "How long has your friend known Heywood?"

"They were together in Salt Lake City before coming out here about six months back," Slocum said. "I don't know how long they were partners before."

"You weren't with them? With Heywood and Sanders?"

"I knew Sanders just before he wanted to leave to go prospecting. He's got quite a silver tongue and talked me into loaning him money I didn't exactly have."

"What do you mean?"

"I talked a bit too big. I borrowed the money so I wouldn't look like I had promised something to Sanders I could not deliver." Slocum thought glumly about the trouble he had gotten himself into by borrowing the money from Jenks.

"So you just knew him casually?"

"I ended up with more than I reckoned for. The Lucky Lady is a fountain spewing out gold ore faster than we can smelt it."

"You didn't know Heywood or Yarrow?"

"Yarrow? I just heard that name a week back when Sanders mentioned him. I've never laid eyes on the man," Slocum said. He felt as if a sheriff were accusing him of some crime.

"I didn't think you would have. Go on, John. I'll see you at the cemetery tomorrow." Sarah June smiled but her eyes had a distant look now, as if she saw horizons he never could.

Slocum paid his respects and joined Sanders, glad he was riding while his partner had to drive the wagon. It was easier to stay upwind by trotting a few yards away from the wagon.

16

The turnout at the funeral was larger than Slocum expected, but then he saw that most of the men were angling to stand beside the new widow. Women were a scarce commodity in Aurum and letting one go to waste because her husband had met an untimely end was not possible for many of the men.

Betty stood with her arm linked with the land agent's. Slocum saw that the man wore a block on one shoe. His right leg was a good inch shorter than his left, probably from some accident and a doctor that couldn't properly patch him up. Wilhelmina and her husband stood apart, on the far side of the grave. The tall blonde looked upset. Her husband stared down into the grave as if he saw himself in the coffin rather than Heywood.

Being one of the few in town who could read, the barkeep from a saloon down on the main street said a few words from the Bible. Nobody paid much attention. They were too busy ogling Sarah June. The widow stood silently, dressed in black but looking as lovely as a summer sunflower. She might have worn widow's weeds, but there was nothing sad about her expression. Slocum saw that she kept an eye on Wilhelmina during the entire service.

"Any of you galoots want to say anything more?" the barkeep asked.

"Reckon I do," said Wilhelmina's man. "Me and Heywood, well, we weren't always on the best of terms, but we came from Salt Lake City together to make our fortunes. We did mighty good. We both have good-hearted, decent women. Or Heywood *did*. Now he's got nuthin'. He's just worm food."

Slocum saw Sarah June's reaction when the man spoke. Her jaw tightened, and she looked as if she would jump over the grave and rip out the man's throat. But she stood and stared, her blue eyes glacially cold.

"He's got nuthin', and I got me one fine woman. Just like Heywood had," the man rushed on.

Slocum nudged Sanders and asked, "The one with Wilhelmina—what's his name?"

"Yarrow," Sanders said. Somehow, this did not surprise Slocum.

"He's another of your partners?"

"Don't fret, Slocum," Sanders said. "I bought him out, too. You're half owner of the Lucky Lady."

"Any more partners around here?"

"Not around here. Got another back in Salt Lake City, but don't reckon I'll ever see Carson again."

Heywood, Yarrow, and one other. Slocum considered so many partners to be a few too many, unless you were robbing banks. He touched the quarter of the silver dollar he had taken off the dead man shot just after he and the four women had left Salt Lake City. The Silver Dollar Gang.

"Rest in peace, Heywood," Yarrow said. "Or burn in hell. Whatever it is, we'll all be seein' you soon enough."

"Thanks for those inspiring words, brother," the bartender said sarcastically. "Now get the dirt thrown in on top of him 'fore the buzzards swoop down on him. And the first drink's on me!"

A wild whoop of glee went up as the miners quickly left,

but not before stopping to take Sarah June's hand in their own grimy paws and assure her they would be more than willing to do what they could to help her through her time of sorrow.

Slocum hung back while Sanders went on into town with the crowd. He wanted a word with Sarah June, but the woman had gone to Wilhelmina and the two women were arguing. Slocum caught only a word now and then, and none of it made a great deal of sense. Whatever Sarah June said caused Wilhelmina to shake her head furiously, point, and say loud enough for him to hear, "There is no way! You are not right!"

Wilhelmina pushed Sarah June away and rushed to her husband. Or husband-to-be. Slocum was not sure how to characterize the man who had won her in the spirited auction. Yarrow and Wilhelmina made a wide detour around Sarah June, got into a buggy, and rattled off. This gave Slocum the opportunity to speak to Sarah June.

"Sorry about the funeral," Slocum said. "If I'd known that was all there would be, I would have said some words myself."

"But you didn't know him, John. You said so."

"Funerals aren't for the dead," Slocum said. "They're for the living. You're right that I didn't know Heywood. Never met him. But I could have done better to comfort you."

"I'm sure you could," Sarah June said, her voice softening and her eyes welling with tears for the first time.

"You didn't find much sympathy with Wilhelmina. You two have a falling-out?"

"Something like that," Sarah June said, her mood shifting mercurially again. She was again cold and distant.

"Could I see you back to the mine or are you going to stay in town?"

"There's no need, John. I can take care of myself. Really."

"Are you sure you want to be alone at a time like this?"

"What exactly are you offering?"

"Someone to listen if you want to talk. Nothing more." Slocum knew the entanglements a man could get himself into taking up with a new widow. Truth was, Sarah June hardly qualified to be quite an entanglement. She and Heywood had been together for only a handful of days. Slocum and Sarah June had ridden side by side on the way from Utah for a far longer time. His thoughts about her had been anything but noble, and if he was any judge, hers were even more licentious.

"I'll be fine. Why don't you go on into town and have that free drink? You look as if you could use it to get the dust out of your throat." She grabbed his arm as he turned to go. "Thank you, John. You've been right kind to a stranger like me."

"You make it sound final, like we won't see each other again."

Sarah June smiled, but there was neither sadness nor pleasure. It was more the expression on a hungry wolf.

"The future is always uncertain." She stood on tiptoe and gave him a quick kiss on the cheek, then left without another word. Slocum watched her get into her buggy and drive away. He shook his head. For a town that thrived on gold mining and nothing else, life was certainly complicated.

Too complicated for his liking. As he walked into town from the cemetery, Slocum considered asking Lemuel to buy him out. In fact, he had already decided that was what he wanted. Lemuel Sanders would come out ahead, owning outright a profitable gold mine. Slocum would have money galore to spend as he made his way from one town to the next, hunting for what he could never find—contentment. Happiness was too elusive to ever find, but he had settled on contentment as a decent goal.

In his way, he had found it. On the trail. Under the stars. Going where the wind blew him. Being no man's servant.

Having no servants of his own. Slocum got contentment out of being free.

He headed for the saloon with the crowd spilling out the front doors. That had to be the one giving free drinks. As he approached, the miners parted for him, recognizing that he had helped Sanders recover Heywood's body. Or maybe he still stank of the corpse. Slocum found Sanders at the far end of the bar, knocking back one drink after another.

"You're taking Heywood's death mighty hard," Slocum said. "Or is this just a chance to cadge free whiskey?"

"Got a bad feeling, Slocum," his partner said. "She killed him. I'm sure of it."

Slocum said nothing. He suspected Sarah June knew more about how her husband had died than she was letting on. Her lack of grief was one thing. She hardly knew Heywood, after all, even if she had been pledged to him. But the way she had stared into the grave at the funeral and the way she acted otherwise told Slocum she was delighted that Heywood had died. Might have been a poor start to the marriage and she was not inclined to speak poorly of the dead, but he doubted that. Something more was going on.

"Tell me about Yarrow," Slocum said suddenly.

Sanders looked up, fury blossoming on his face.

"Go to hell. Him and me and Heywood, we came to Aurum to get rich. I did. Yarrow's not bad off. Heywood was the least of us."

"What happened in Salt Lake City?"

"Nothing." Sanders knocked back another shot. When he put the shot glass on the bar, he wobbled a mite. Slocum knew how much liquor his partner could drink before reaching this stage. Another couple drinks and Sanders would be drunker than a lord and meaner than a stepped-on rattler.

"What'll you give me for my share of the Lucky Lady?"

For a moment, Sanders was shocked into sobriety. Then he grabbed the bottle and didn't even bother with the glass.

He took a draught out of it long enough to get falling-down drunk.

"You talkin' nonsense again? You want to get rich. Alongside me. That's a good claim, Slocum, and you know it."

"I'm getting itchy feet," Slocum said. "This town's too big."

"There's not a hunnerd pip-people in it." Sanders was starting to slur his words. "Can't go. Need you to watch my back."

"What happened in Salt Lake City?" Slocum saw the anger blaze up again, but this time when it died, fear replaced it.

"Hey, you two. Lemme through. Sanders, Slocum, got somethin' to tell you!"

Slocum saw Betty's land agent hobbling toward them. He looked agitated. Slocum took a deep breath and let it out slowly. The longer he stayed in Aurum, the more complicated things got. Whatever Franklin Fremont wanted to tell them, it was not going to be pleasant.

"My missus wants a word with you two."

Slocum looked at Sanders and knew he was in no condition.

"What's she want? I'll talk to her."

Fremont saw the wisdom in what Slocum said and immediately turned and began pushing through the throng of miners again until they reached the boardwalk outside the saloon. Betty stood there, fidgeting. Her face lit up when she saw Slocum.

"John, thank goodness," she said. "I was afraid you wouldn't do it."

"What are you talking about? He never said why you wanted to see me."

Betty shot Fremont a dark look, then took Slocum by the arm and steered him away from the saloon door to where they could talk more privately.

"It's Wilhelmina. She's missing."

"Missing? It hasn't been an hour since the funeral. How missing could she be in that time?"

"I . . . I went after her. I found their buggy, but they were both gone."

"Her and Yarrow?"

"Please, John, put my mind at ease. Go find her. For me. For old times."

"There aren't any 'old times,'" Slocum said. "Why do you think she's come to harm?"

"A feeling," Betty said. There was more, but the woman couldn't bring herself to say it. Slocum saw her start a couple times, then lapse into silence.

"I'll do it, but this is the end. No more."

"You've looked after all four of us like we were your . . . family."

Slocum knew Betty had started to say "wives."

He snorted in disgust and went to get his horse. Slocum wondered if he ought to sign over his rights in the Lucky Lady to Fremont and then just keep riding. Let Betty deal with Sanders—or Sanders deal with the feisty brunette. As he rode out of town, heading toward Yarrow's claim, he wondered why he felt any obligation at all to the women. Preen had paid him in Salt Lake City to deliver the four. Only three got to Aurum, but Tabitha had willingly stayed back in Braden. His job was done. He wasn't the women's keeper.

He wasn't their husband, either.

Before he had gone two miles, Slocum drew rein and stared at the evidence in the road. Most of the snow had melted, leaving behind mud that didn't take tracks well. From what little he could see, the buggy had slewed off the road and tumbled down an embankment. Slocum dismounted and went to the verge of the road. The marks on the mountainside were plain. He caught sight of a buggy wheel poking up from where it had caught on some brush.

Before he risked life and limb going down to see if anyone had survived, he scouted the area.

"Now isn't that something?" he muttered to himself. Two sets of prints left the edge of the drop-off. One set went back to the road, and he lost the other within a few feet because of the rocky terrain. He looked up when he heard the clatter of chains and the creak of leather. An old rig pulled by the most dilapidated-looking horse he had ever seen came down the road.

Slocum stepped out and waved. He could use some help. Then he saw the driver's face. Yarrow.

"Howdy," Yarrow called. "You're Slocum, ain't you? Lemuel's new partner."

"What happened here?" Slocum pointed to the spot where the buggy had gone over the side.

"Me and the missus was comin' back from the funeral when a wheel started wobbling and then threw us out. The buggy, along with a perfectly good horse, went over the brink."

"Threw the two of you out?"

"My missus wasn't up to hikin', so I went on up to the claim and got this nag so I could drive her back."

"Where is Wilhelmina?"

Yarrow looked around. The panic on his face told the story.

"Wili! Wilhelmina! Where are you hidin'? Come on out. It's jist me and that Slocum fella!"

"You left her alone?"

"Why not? Most of the real roughnecks would be at the bar gettin' theyselves drunk. Nobody'd be on this road, and Wilhelmina was feelin' mighty low."

"Did you tell her to stay put?"

"She's not dumb. She'd know to do that."

"Let's hunt for her. I don't see any trace of her after she walked to that stretch of rock." Slocum pointed to where the smaller footprints had gone. He looked up into the rocks where the stawberry blonde woman might have taken cover.

There was no good reason for her to hide, but she had left the road and was nowhere to be seen.

"Wili! Where are you? Dammit, come on out!" Yarrow stormed into the maze of boulders while Slocum held back. If Yarrow flushed her, Slocum wanted to see if she ran to find a new hiding place or if she simply came out. As Yarrow had pointed out, Wilhelmina was not a stupid woman. She had gone into the rocks for a reason, and the best one Slocum could figure was to hide.

From what? Who? Yarrow? Someone else?

He began studying the stretch of road past the point where the buggy wheel had come off. He wasn't able to verify Yarrow's account, but the mud had pretty well swallowed up most of the evidence. Only by pulling the buggy up could he tell if the wheel had come off or if everything Yarrow said was a lie. But why would he kill Wilhelmina? He seemed devoted enough to her. The way they had stood close together at the funeral told Slocum there hadn't been any bad blood between them then. Had they argued on the way back to their mine?

There was no way he could tell. But he thought he found faint tracks of another buggy. The mud swallowed up any real evidence, though.

Yarrow came back, looking more distraught than before.

"I can't find her. She ain't no place to be found!"

"How many folks drive buggies along this road?"

"Just us. Most of the miners have buckboards. Some share. It ain't cheap buyin' and keepin' a rig."

"See anybody else on this road today?"

"Jist you, Slocum."

Even as he stared at the faint traces he had found— thought he had found—the melting snow and warmth from the Colorado sun erased everything. If he had not known Yarrow's buggy had gone over at this spot, he would no longer have been able to tell.

"You thinkin' someone gave her a ride? Not to my mine, they didn't!"

"Where's the road go?" Slocum pointed ahead.

"A few claims up that way. Mostly petered-out mines."

Slocum's mind raced. If someone had followed Yarrow and Wilhelmina, they might have taken the woman on up into the hills to one of the working mines. Or to an abandoned one. Wilhelmina was a mighty fine-looking woman, and the miners were horny bastards.

"Somebody took her. Ain't that it, Slocum? That what you see here?"

"I don't see squat," Slocum said. "This mud's useless for giving any trace."

"I got to find her. This is awful!"

"Tell you what, Yarrow. Go scout a ways up the road for any sign of a buggy. If you don't see anything, go back to your mine. I'll meet you there."

"Where're you goin', Slocum?"

"Need to go back to town," he said. "Soon as I get some supplies, I'll come on back. I suspect you and Wilhelmina will be all cozied up by the stove and my trip will be for nothing."

Yarrow nodded, reassured. But Slocum doubted Yarrow would find anything. And he had never asked what supplies Slocum needed.

Slocum figured he needed a box or two of ammunition. At least.

17

"You want what, Mr. Slocum?" Franklin Fremont looked confused.

"You're the land agent, aren't you? You register claims."

"Even do a little assay work since the chemists over in Grand Junction take forever and charge so much. Folks around here want their results quick."

"I want a map of the area around Yarrow's mine. Do you have it or not?"

"A map? Well, not exactly. All I do is record what the miners tell me."

Slocum wanted to strangle the man, but Betty stood close by and would not have permitted it. Exasperated, he asked again for a map of the countryside.

"Well, I've got this one. Shows where all the hills and ravines are, but it's not got many mines marked on it." Fremont spread the map on the counter. Slocum shoved his finger down and followed the road toward Yarrow's claim.

"Here. What's this? A smudge, or is it something else?"

Fremont peered at the wavy line Slocum indicated.

"Looks to be a ravine. Must be a good-sized one, since it's on the map. Why put small arroyos on a map?"

"The map was made by the man who had this job before you?"

"Mr. Latham, yes. He was a cranky old bastard." Fremont turned and smiled weakly. "Sorry for the salty language, my dear." He turned back to Slocum. "Mr. Latham considered maps a hobby."

Slocum wasn't listening any longer. The ravine must be wide, and it worked around the far side of the hill where Yarrow's claim had been staked. If what Fremont said was right, most of the mines in the area were abandoned, letting anyone who wanted to ride unnoticed around the hill and go straight to the Sombrero mine in the next valley over. Wilhelmina might have taken this route and gone to see Sarah June. If so, no one would have spotted her. But why would she want to talk secretly? Slocum knew he might be making a mountain from a molehill. This was a shorter route than coming back to Aurum and then going to the Sombrero. Time, distance—those might have been the reasons Wilhelmina would have chosen to continue around the hill to see Sarah June.

If she had even gone to see the other woman.

"Mind if I keep the map?" Slocum asked, folding the page and tucking it into his pocket.

"Well, I must protest. That is an official record and—"

"Franklin." Betty simply spoke the man's name and he shut up. He looked glum at the prospect of the map leaving his office, but his wife had spoken.

"How's the claim coming for your mine?" Slocum had to ask.

"It appears that the Dead Man's Revenge will be mine, since Rafe's partners have hightailed it."

"Funny how threat of a necktie party can do that," Slocum said. Betty looked at him appraisingly.

"Isn't it, John? You really must come out and join Franklin and me for dinner sometime."

"Betty decided to rename the mine," cut in Fremont. "I insisted we call it the Bountiful Betty."

"A good choice," Slocum said. He left the land office and looked at the sky. The sun was starting to sink in the west. He had buried a man in the morning and promised to find a lost woman by noon. Now he had to get back in the saddle and make good on that last promise. Somehow, he thought, the funeral and the disappearance were tied together. The memory of Sarah June talking with Wilhelmina stuck in his mind. He almost rode for the Sombrero mine, but he had told Yarrow he would be back.

Who knew? Yarrow might have found Wilhelmina wandering around the countryside and have her beside a nice fire, warming up.

Slocum turned his collar to the increasingly biting wind coming off the higher elevations and rode for Yarrow's claim. He reached the mine just after sundown.

"Yarrow!" he called. "I'm back from town." Slocum had his map, and his saddlebags were full of ammunition and grub, in case the search for Wilhelmina lengthened into days instead of a few hours. He saw the dilapidated wagon and tired horse near the cabin.

Slocum paused and listened hard. Then he took a deep sniff of the cold mountain air. He heard nothing but the expected noises. The horses. The settling of the timbers in the mine. Distant wind whispering through the pines. His nose caught that pine scent and more than a hint of a badly kept outhouse.

He did not hear any other humans nor did he smell burning wood. If Wilhelmina had returned, Yarrow would have fixed a fire.

Slocum pulled his six-shooter and went to the cabin. The door stood open.

"You in there, Yarrow? It's me. Slocum." He kicked the door fully open and spun into the room. He lifted his six-gun and then tucked it back into his holster. There was no need to be worried about Yarrow. The man lay sprawled on the floor, a bullet hole between his eyes. Slocum knelt and examined the body. The single bullet had killed him instantly. The best he could make out, Yarrow had gone to the door, opened it when someone had knocked, and then he had been shot. He took one step away and fell like cut timber.

Slocum looked around but saw nothing out of place. Whoever had killed Yarrow had shot him and left.

Going back to the body, Slocum noticed that the top button on the man's shirt had been ripped off. He pressed his fingers down into the cold flesh and then traced out a red mark starting at the sides of Yarrow's neck and circling around to the back. He had worn something on a leather thong that had been ripped off.

Slocum reconsidered his ideas of what had happened. Yarrow was shot, fell, then someone had entered, gripped the necklace, and yanked hard enough to tear it off. Then they had left.

Fumbling in his pocket, Slocum pulled out the quarter of a silver dollar he had found on the dead man just outside Salt Lake City. It had a hole drilled in it, as if it had, at one time, been worn on a necklace.

"The Silver Dollar Gang," Slocum said. He remembered Sanders talking about secret societies and symbols.

He stood and left the cabin and its corpse. Anything he considered, including that Yarrow, Heywood, and the dead man along the trail had been in the gang with Lemuel Sanders, was just speculation.

"Carson," he said. "The man's name was Carson." Slocum held up the quarter silver dollar and flipped it, capturing the light of a waxing moon. "This was yours, wasn't it, Carson?"

The rising wind was his only answer. Slocum tucked the piece of silver dollar back into his pocket and began searching the area around the cabin. He had not expected to find anything, but tracks in a snowbank led off toward the woods. Slocum tried to decipher the footprints and couldn't. Probably two people, one following in the footprints of the other. Whether this was for convenience or had been intended to hide the tracks, he could not tell. He went into the woods and lost the trail several times in the intense darkness. More than once he lit a lucifer and hastily scanned the ground. The way the slope increased dramatically warned Slocum that he was nearing a cliff.

The trees grew right up to the brink. The few feet of rock between the trees and the drop-off refused to give up any information. He edged closer to the cliff and then chanced a look down. He closed his eyes for a moment, then took a longer, better look.

In stark contrast to the white snow lay a woman dressed in black. The dark splotches around her had to be blood. In the moonlight blood always looked like ink. Try as he might Slocum could not identify the woman, but it had to be either Sarah June or Wilhelmina.

He backed off, then spent the next two hours finding a path down to the foot of the cliff. As he approached, he saw right away that it was Wilhelmina who had died. He looked up and shuddered. That was a long fall. More than long enough for the woman to think about dying. Slocum examined Wilhelmina's body the best he could, but the impact had left her broken in more places than he could count. That she had landed faceup was the only way he could identify her.

Slocum had brought rope with him and a hunk of canvas from the mine. He rolled Wilhelmina onto the thick tarp, then trussed her up. Trying to drag her proved too difficult. As distasteful as it was, Slocum heaved the body onto his shoulder and staggered off. It was a long, difficult climb back to the cabin. He laid Wilhelmina next to Yarrow, then fixed himself some coffee.

It settled in his belly and made him nauseous. He finally

shut the cabin door, got his bedroll, and found a spot outside where he could stretch out and get a few hours' sleep. Just after dawn he came awake, loaded the bodies into the wagon, and drove to Aurum.

"Might be a better occupation," the barkeep said. "Servin' tarantula juice is profitable, but I make a hell of a lot more sayin' words over the dead."

"Just get on with it," Slocum said. He was tired of funerals. It was especially exhausting that one of the two being buried was a woman he had been hired to protect.

"It's not your fault, John," Betty said quietly. "We all got to Aurum and you could have moved on right away. This would have still happened, whether you stayed in town or not."

"I know," Slocum said. He touched the piece of the silver dollar in his pocket. He knew how to find the killer—it was whoever was starting a collection of the silver pieces. The one he now carried he had found under the body along the road—the killer had not been able to find it. Or had been too squeamish to roll Carson over and hunt for it.

But she was learning. The killer was getting bolder, more vicious.

"You were in town, weren't you?"

"What? Why, yes, of course. I was helping Franklin with some of the paperwork. It does get to be a burden."

"I thought so." Slocum doubted Tabitha had ridden in from Braden. That left only one possible killer. Sarah June stood alone on the far side of the grave. The expression on her face was neutral, but she would make a terrible poker player. Now and then Slocum saw the revealing twitches and grimaces as the barkeep gave the simple service.

Sarah June was trying not to show her glee at this burial.

"Did Sarah June and Wilhelmina have a falling-out?"

"They were never on good terms," Betty said. "Then again, they were better friends to each other than to me."

"Because you bragged so on how I . . . rescued you."

"Yes, thank you for being so discreet." Betty glanced over at Franklin. The man stood quietly, hat in his hand and looking sad. Slocum thought he probably reacted that way at all funerals.

"What do you know of Sarah June before we left Salt Lake City?"

"About as much as I did of the others. All our stories were so similar, it held us together. That might have been why Preen found us such easy pickings."

"Who spoke up first? One of you or Sarah June?"

"She was the most reticent of us about describing what she had endured. From what she said and the parts she was too embarrassed to mention, she might have had it the worst of any of us."

Slocum thought on this for a spell. Sarah June might have listened to the other three women's stories and concocted one of her own that mirrored their experiences. Giving her tale a little more flair would be enough to keep the three from asking too many questions. She was running from Salt Lake City for a reason other than being a junior wife in a harem. What was it? What could be so heinous that she willingly killed three men and a woman who was as close to being a friend as anyone in the world?

"Do you think she needs support, John? Look at her. So drawn and sad."

Slocum stared hard at Sarah June and saw something entirely different. Betty might be affected by Wilhelmina's death, but for Sarah June it was water off a duck's back.

He moved around and stood beside her. She looked up at him, her blue eyes hard as flint.

"He's dead, John."

"Another one," Slocum agreed. "You started with Carson, didn't you?"

Sarah June jumped as if he had stuck her with a pin. Her mouth opened, then closed.

"How did you know?"

"A guess," he admitted.

"You weren't one of them. You weren't. You couldn't have been."

"One of them?" Slocum took out the quarter silver dollar and turned it slowly in front of her so it caught the bright autumn sun.

"You—" Sarah June took a step back and started to open her purse. She stopped and looked hard at him. "You got that off Carson's body."

"How do you know?"

Sarah June opened her purse and fumbled inside. Slocum tensed. She had used a small pistol, probably a derringer, to kill Carson. It would fit easily in her purse. The flash of silver coming out made him reach for his six-shooter, then he stopped. She held two pieces of a silver dollar.

"I am sure they all fit together," Sarah June said.

"You took it off Heywood after you killed him," Slocum said.

"I took it off him before I pushed him into the pit."

"You hit him with a board?"

"I used the rope to catch him. As he was struggling to get the loop off of his ankles, I hit him. Several times." Sarah June turned more distant and cold. "Then I took the piece of the dollar and pushed him into the pit. I think he was dead before, but I wish he had been alive so he could have driven himself crazy trying to escape."

"You really hated him, didn't you?"

"Carson and Yarrow, too."

"You didn't recognize them, though. How can you hate people you've never laid eyes on?"

"I shot him square between the eyes," she said dreamily. She made no effort to answer Slocum's question. He wondered if she could, since she was reliving the killings. "I knocked, he opened the cabin door, and I shot him. Just like that. He stood in the door looking at me. I lifted my gun and pulled the trigger. My only regret is that he did not suffer enough."

"The same pistol you used on Carson?"

Sarah June shrugged. "What if it was?"

"Why did you kill Wilhelmina?"

"I didn't kill her. She saw me shoot Yarrow and ran off. I tried to stop her, but she did not know where she was going. Or she was so frightened that she got lost. She slipped and fell to her death. I regret that. I didn't much like her, but I meant her no harm."

"You only wanted to kill her husband."

"She's better off. Either without him or dead, she's better off than living with that son of a bitch."

"What did the Silver Dollar Gang do to you?"

"Nothing. Not a damned thing." She pushed past him. "Excuse me, John. I must tend to business."

"Are you done with the killing?"

"I prefer to think of them as executions." She jerked free when he took her arm. When she saw he was not going to let her go, she called out, "Please join me in a tribute to these wonderful people. At the saloon, if our preacher will be so good as to pour. And would some of you care to escort me?"

The miners rushed over and crowded Slocum out. Sarah June went with them, in the middle of a crowd he could never hope to push through. But there was no hurry. Slocum knew who was left on her death roll.

18

Slocum bided his time outside the saloon. He could have used a drink or two, especially if someone else was paying, but he wanted to keep his head clear. When Lemuel Sanders stumbled out, Slocum corralled him and shoved him down into a chair on the boardwalk.

"I want you to buy me out," Slocum said. "Now."

"What's your hurry? You're so all-fired het up to leave Aurum when there's a fortune to be had, it makes me wonder 'bout you, Slocum."

"I want to go. Now."

"No money. None on me. If you wait till tomorrow when the bank opens, I'll give you whatever's there. We can call it even."

Slocum frowned. What passed for a bank in Aurum was a corner of the general store. The owner kept a lockbox. Mostly he ran a set of books detailing what gold was brought in and how much the miners owed him for supplies they had already bought. Nobody used him as a true bank. Otherwise, there would have been road agents lined up all the way out of town waiting to rob the place.

"How much?" Slocum asked.

"Maybe five hundred. And you can get credit at the

store. Toss that into the pot and stir. You could use a new blanket for your horse. Ole Ned's got a nice one he traded some Injun for. And grub for the trail. Jerky. Canned tomatoes and peaches."

"Sounds good," Slocum said. If he got five hundred in gold dust to go with the nearly eight hundred he had already taken from the mine, he would be more than happy. Mining was hard work, even if he was making as much as a hundred dollars a day at it.

"What's lit the fire under your ass?"

"Sarah June," Slocum said. "Has she been talking to you?"

"She's sweet on another fellow. A guy who came to town 'bout the same time I did."

"From Utah?"

"Don't rightly know and it doesn't matter. She's not likely to be keeping my bed warm." Sanders closed one eye to focus better as he squinted at Slocum. "She any good when it comes to mountin' 'n' ridin'?"

"She's mighty good at roping," Slocum said, remembering what Sarah June had said about hog-tying Heywood before she clobbered him with the board and dumped him into the pit.

"Heard tell some folks like that," Sanders said. He belched loudly and wobbled, although he was still securely seated in the chair.

"Who's the man she's talking to?"

"Can't remember his name. Skinny little runt. Don't look like he's got an ounce of muscle on him, but he can work all day and half the night. Might be he's part Chinee. They can do that, you know. Work without stopping, 'cept to eat a bowl of rice."

Slocum left Sanders drifting off into his alcoholic fog. The man was so close to being pickled he was no good.

Slocum had no reason to stay in Aurum. The money for the mine meant nothing to him compared to being away from the tornado whirling about, but he wanted to stop Sarah June before she got in worse trouble. She had not been a cold-blooded killer when they met up in Salt Lake City. She was becoming one fast, and it was not for personal gain. Slocum knew the Sombrero mine was profitable but required full-time working.

It was a fool's errand, but Slocum had to talk Sarah June out of any more killing. He pushed his way into the saloon and looked around. It had surprised him that she had wanted to go inside, but then it got her closer to her next victim. He stood on a table and looked around. He did not see her. If she had been anywhere inside, there would have been a tight knot of miners surrounding her.

"You lookin' fer the blonde girl?"

"Where'd she go?" Slocum looked down at a young man hardly old enough to shave.

"I tried to get close to her, but she slipped out the back way 'bout a half hour ago."

"Anyone with her?"

"Not that I could see. Uh, mister, you know her, don't you?"

Slocum said nothing. The young man looked suddenly embarrassed.

"You put in a good word fer me with her? I kin work that mine of hers till my hands are bloody."

Slocum knew the man wanted to do more than work the mine, but he assured the youngster that he would. He hopped down and backed out of the saloon. Lemuel Sanders was passed out in the chair on the boardwalk.

Wasting no time, Slocum got his horse and mounted. For a moment, he worried that Sarah June had led her next victim from the saloon, but he saw where she had halted her buggy. Only one set of footprints led to where it had been parked—small prints. She might be meeting the man somewhere. The only place Slocum could think of was back at the Sombrero. As he rode along, trying to keep the buggy tracks in view, he saw that he was probably right. Sarah June was going out of town in the direction of the mine.

He urged his horse to a trot. If she had left only a half hour before him, he could overtake her before . . .

Before what? Before she killed again? If she was bound and determined to keep on killing, if she had developed a taste for it, there was nothing Slocum could do to stop her short of wringing her neck. For some reason, he didn't think he was up to that. If he exposed her to the townsfolk, they weren't likely to stick her head into a noose, either. Not when she was the only unmarried woman in town.

All she would have to do was bat her eyelashes at a jury, and they would fall all over themselves to acquit her. And Slocum could not blame them. Something told him the reason for her killing spree was mighty good, but that didn't mean he could let her keep going. When he dug down to the bottom of all his reasons, he found himself caring about what happened to her.

Slocum turned up the road leading to the mine. The buggy tracks were fresh in the dirt now. He reached the cabin in time to see a puff of black smoke rise out of the chimney. Sarah June had arrived only a few minutes ahead of him.

He hit the ground and went to the door. He slowed, then called out, "Sarah June, it's me, Slocum. I want to talk."

The door opened. She looked pale and drawn, but she smiled just a little when she saw him.

"Do come in, John. I wasn't expecting you."

"Were you expecting someone else?" He reached over and lifted her right hand. She had a derringer clutched in it. She pulled away and turned her back to him.

"This is dangerous country. You know that."

"It's dangerous because of you. You've killed repeatedly."

"I had to," she said, spinning and facing him. "I want every last one of those raping murderers dead!"

Slocum said nothing. Sarah June's cheeks burned now with the intensity of her emotion. Her jaw was set, and her lips had pulled back into a feral snarl.

"She was my sister. They raped her for hours, then killed her."

"The Silver Dollar Gang?"

"Yes." Sarah June's answer was more like a hiss from a rattlesnake than a word.

"You're sure it was them?"

"Oh, yes, I'm sure. They left their calling card." She spun and went to her valise. She searched through it a few seconds and pulled out a silver dollar. "This was jammed up . . . up her—" Sarah June broke out crying. She sagged and then sat heavily on the bed. "What they did to her was terrible. The undertaker found the silver dollar and showed it to the federal marshal. He said it wasn't the first time. Others. They had done that to other women and bragged on it."

"The marshal couldn't find them," Slocum said, "because they hightailed it out of town."

"All but Carson. I have no idea why he stayed. I got on his trail, then lost it. But I found that the others had come to Aurum."

"And you heard about Betty and the others coming here?"

"Mail-order brides—it sounded so perverted. But I would do anything to bring the monsters to justice who had killed Mary Beth. The only thing was, I didn't have any money and I knew I could never make it here on my own."

"Preen furnished both."

"Carson must have gotten wind of me leaving and tried to kill me. I got him instead." She held up her derringer and stared at it. "Killing him was hard. I knew what a disgusting man he was, but it was hard."

"That's why you didn't find his quarter of a silver dollar."

"You found it. But I had to hide what I'd done. From you and from the others."

"You did a good job," Slocum said.

Sarah June sniffed and smiled weakly. "Is that a compliment?"

"Take it however you want," Slocum said.

"As we got closer to Aurum, I knew what I had to do. Not marrying someone would make me the talk of the town—or an outcast. So I did what I had to and found the others who had been in the gang. I didn't know what they looked like, but they carried the pieces of the silver dollar."

Sarah June looked up at Slocum. Her blue eyes welled with tears now and she began to sob harder.

"Tell me I did the right thing, John. Tell me I'm not as horrible as those raping, murdering sons of bitches!"

He sat beside her on the bed and gently took the pistol from her hand. He laid it on a nearby table. Then Slocum took her in his arms.

"You did what you had to. Are you done killing?"

"Don't make me promise anything, John. I won't. My sister's memory demands that I—"

Slocum kissed her trembling lips. For a heartbeat, Sarah June was motionless. Then she hungrily returned the kiss.

She broke off, gasping out, "I've wanted to do that from the minute I laid eyes on you, John. But you and Betty—"

"I was always saving her. If you had needed me more . . ."

"I need you now."

Slocum kissed her again. Her body pressed hotly against his. Somehow, he worked his way out of his coat and vest. Sarah June worked to get him out of his shirt. He dropped his gun belt to the floor as she fumbled to open the button on his jeans.

"Oh," she said, seeing his erection snapping out at attention. "I had no idea."

"You're not a virgin," Slocum said.

"No, no, I meant I had no idea you were so huge. No wonder Betty was bragging about you and her and—"

Slocum quieted her again with another kiss that worked from her lips around to her ear. He thrust his tongue into the channel of her ear, hinting at repeating the same motion lower, with different organs meeting and merging. She clung to him fiercely. Slocum kissed down to her earlobe and around to her throat. Sarah June threw her head back to give him full access.

His mouth moved lower yet, to the top of her breasts. He fumbled about for a few seconds releasing her blouse and letting her succulent white mounds come tumbling free. He buried his face between them. Licking and kissing, he worked around the base of each breast, tracing out a figure eight. Then he worked slowly to the crest of her left tit. He sucked in the firm, rubbery nub and tongued it hard.

Sarah June moaned softly at his oral attack. When he abandoned that breast, he leapfrogged immediately to the other. As he suckled there, he cupped the other and massaged, stroked, and fondled until Sarah June wilted. He followed her back down to the bed. His mouth never rested as he worked all over her chest. Then he worked lower.

"Oh, yes, John. I want this so. I've wanted it from—oh!"

He did not want talk. He wanted action. Hot and hard and heavy action. His hands slid under her skirts and pushed them up around her waist. He found the tangled damp mat nestled between her legs and began stroking his fingers over it. When he parted her nether lips and ran up and down, he got his hand soaked with her inner oils.

When he pressed down at the tiny little pink spire poking up at the top of the V of her sex lips, Sarah June lifted her hips from the bed and ground them down into his hand.

"I want you, John. I want you inside me so!"

He moved rapidly. The ache in his balls had spread into his loins until he was at the point of exploding like a stick of dynamite. Sarah June was lovely, she was willing, she needed him as much as he needed her. He crouched between her upraised legs. Her knees curled up. He slid his arms under her knees and bent her double, opening her wantonly.

"Yes, yes, do it, John. I want it so!"

His hips moved forward. He felt the soft pressure and heat as he touched her. Then he sank in a few inches and gasped. He was surrounded by tightness that squeezed down firmly all around. Slowly pushing the rest of the way, he felt the woman begin to respond furiously. Her hips began bucking and she ground her crotch into his, trying to take him even deeper into her. He obliged. He leaned forward, using his greater weight to drive himself balls deep.

"Oh, John, you're so big. Move, damn you, ride me hard."

He slid his hand down and cupped her breasts, squeezing them as he thrust in and out of her with deliberate strokes. All about him the heat mounted. Her juices leaked out around the thick plug of his cock. But the heat! She was burning him up. He began moving with greater speed. This provoked her to even greater movement under him.

She bucked and thrashed about like a wild bronco. He abandoned his posts on her breasts and reached around her, grabbing the twin moons of her ass. He lifted and kneaded and tried to pull her body entirely into his.

He sank even deeper. But what drove him wild with need was the way her strong inner muscles grabbed and released him—hot, moist, tight. He began thrusting faster until the heat building up along his entire length threatened to burn him to a nubbin. Deep within his loins he felt the rising tides and fought to contain them. He wanted this to last forever.

Looking down into Sarah June's face made him want to stay this way, right now, here, hidden away fully within her tightness, forever and ever. Her eyes were closed and she tossed her head from side to side, leaving a halo of her bright blonde hair on the bed. Vagrant beams of light caught her hair and turned it into spun gold.

She muttered incoherently in her lust. The sound of her moans and the feel of her collapsing all about him pushed Slocum over the brink. The rising flood within him suddenly broke through his control and spewed forth. He pumped furiously, and she took every drop until she cried out in release and then sank down under him.

Her blue eyes flickered open. It took a moment for them to focus. When they did, she also had a tiny smile on her lips.

"Thank you, John."

"What are you thanking me for? That was my treat."

"We both needed that," she said. Sarah June turned her head to the side and looked suddenly sad. "Would you mind going? Please?"

Slocum pushed out of the V of her legs and sat on the edge of the bed.

"What are you going to do?"

"I don't know," she said.

"You're not a killer."

"I am," she said fiercely. "I am! But I don't want to be."

"Then let it ride."

"How can I?"

Slocum had no answer for that. He pulled up his jeans, then finished dressing in silence. After strapping on his gun belt, he said, "I'm riding on." He was not sure what he wanted from her. In a way he hoped she would ask to go with him.

She didn't.

Slocum left without another word, got on his horse, and returned to Aurum. All the way he thought furiously about Sarah June's blood feud with the Silver Dollar Gang— about the four who had raped and killed her sister. She had found three of them. Slocum knew the fourth.

He reached the saloon where he had left Lemuel Sanders sitting outside. His partner was gone, but he had not drifted far. Slocum heard the man's voice inside as he sang too loud and too off-key for human ears to tolerate.

Slocum had no trouble sidling up to the bar. Sanders was alone and serenading no one in particular. The large crowd from earlier in the day had disappeared, leaving

only the serious drinkers—the miners with gold dust to
pay for their whiskey.

"Come on over, Slocum. You got a powerful lot of
catching up to do."

Slocum motioned for a drink. The barkeep poured him
one, then slid along the back bar a discreet distance. Slocum
guessed the barkeep might be able to hear what was said, so
he kept his voice low.

"I got to know, Lem."

"The money? Hell, yes, I'll buy you out, Slocum. Don't
want a partner who doesn't intend to get rich."

"To hell with the money," Slocum said. "I have to
know." He reached in his pocket and pulled out the quarter
of a silver dollar he had taken off Carson. "Do you have
one that matches?"

"Right here," Sanders said, tearing his pocket as he
pulled out a piece that fit snugly with the one Slocum had
laid on the bar.

"You raped and killed a woman in Salt Lake City, didn't
you?"

"Did a lot back there. One reason I was so het up to
leave. The others, Yarrow and Heywood, they enjoyed it.
Carson left 'fore we really got down to the good stuff."

"Good stuff?"

"I had that last blonde bitch a couple times. But it was
Heywood that killed her. Told him not to waste a whore
like that."

"You're drunk," Slocum said.

"In my cups," Sanders agreed. "And thinking on the
good times. Those were the good times."

Slocum touched the butt of his six-shooter and then
pulled his hand back. This wasn't his fight.

"Wire me what you will as my share of the Lucky Lady.
I'll be in Denver." Slocum figured he could cross the Front
Range at Mosquito Pass before the heavy snows began to
fall and blocked the way.

"You don't even want to stay till tomorrow? The money's at the—"

"Wire it to me. Whatever you think is fair. I can't stand it here any longer."

"Your loss," Sanders said.

Slocum started to offer Sanders some free advice, then decided not to. He had never known Sanders that well, but such a brutal crime would be punished eventually. It just wasn't Slocum's place to do it.

He mounted and rode due east, letting his horse pick its way along the moonlight trail at its own pace. There was nothing for him here anymore, if there ever had been. Putting as many miles as possible between him and Aurum was more important than stopping for the night.

19

Slocum's horse pulled up lame after four days on the trail. The weather had been good, but the occasional cold rain showers had turned the rocks in the roadway slippery. He was trying to make it up a steep grade without dismounting when his horse got a hoof caught between two slick rocks and stumbled. Slocum was thrown but came up quickly, worried more about his horse than he was his own bruises.

The leg was not broken, but he could not ride the horse without severely—permanently—injuring it. Slocum considered his options. It was more than a week to Denver over increasingly high mountain passes—riding. It was about a week back to Aurum—on foot. Reluctantly, Slocum turned west and began walking. His horse could graze in a mountain meadow for a while. Maybe by the time he returned, the leg would have healed enough for him to catch the horse and lead it on as a pack animal. It might be more humane to simply shoot it, considering how it would be at risk to predatory wolves and coyotes, but Slocum didn't have the heart for that. The pony had served him well and might be able to survive. He owed it that chance.

He took off the bridle and saddle and let the horse roam.

It hobbled a few paces, then, relieved of all weight on its back, trotted off with only a slight limp. It would be fine.

"One foot in front of the other," Slocum said, saddle slung over his shoulder as he began the long trek back to Aurum.

It was closer to ten days later when he trudged into Aurum, footsore and aching all over. The town had not changed in his absence, but he had not expected it to. He went directly to the livery stable and dickered for another horse, which cost twice what it would have in either Denver or Salt Lake City. His deal completed, he went to the general store for supplies.

"Well, if it ain't Mr. Slocum. Didn't expect to see you again," the owner said. "Lem said you up and left all of a sudden. Didn't even want money for your share of the Lucky Lady. You come back for that?"

"No," Slocum said. "Let Sanders keep my share of the mine. He's more interested in getting rich than I ever could be." The words came easily to Slocum. He'd had plenty of time to think on the matter as he returned, and to his surprise it was true. Money was more like an anchor holding him down, especially a lot of it. Better to have enough to do as he pleased, and devil take the hindmost. He had more than enough gold tucked away in his saddlebags to take care of about any need he might have until next spring, even spending freely in Denver.

"That's mighty charitable of you, if I do say so," the owner of the general store said. "Sort of a wedding present, I reckon. A big one, but still a mighty fine wedding present."

Slocum went cold inside.

"Sanders and Sarah June?"

"Reckon so, since she's about the only single woman around, though she's had mighty bad luck with husbands."

"When?" Slocum demanded.

"Why just this morning. They're on their honeymoon 'bout now, I reckon."

"Where? Which mine? The Lucky Lady or the Sombrero?"

"Can't say. As steady a producer as the Sombrero was, the Lucky Lady's a whole lot better. I suspect they'd go to the Lucky Lady, especially now that you're not hanging your hat on a peg there anymore."

Slocum gathered his supplies and went out to stash them in his saddlebags. For the few minutes it took, he debated with himself about going out to the Lucky Lady. What could he hope to do? If Sarah June was going to kill Sanders, she might have done it by now. What if Sanders had figured out who she was and what had brought her to Aurum as a mail-order bride? Was that any better? Or any worse?

He felt an obligation to Sarah June. He felt a different kind to Sanders, since the man had been his partner.

"Had been," Slocum said. "Lem was my partner. Sarah June and I shared a bed once."

He knew his attachment to both went deeper than that. He swung into the saddle, and instead of getting back on the trail for Denver, possibly to lasso his lame horse in that distant meadow, he turned toward the Lucky Lady mine.

Slocum rode steadily, arguing with himself the entire way to the mine. This was none of his business. No matter what. But he felt he had to do something. He just could not figure out what it might be.

The cabin where he had slept and eaten and played cards with Sanders and spun the tales of what to do with all the gold coming from the mine looked as it had when he'd left for the last time. A tiny curl of white smoke came from the chimney, showing someone was inside. Around behind the cabin stood Sarah June's buggy. Three horses and a mule were in the crude corral a bit farther away. The mule brayed and the horses whinnied at his approach.

But from the cabin there was only silence.

He hit the ground and let his reins trail. Going to the door required more guts than he thought he had. No matter what he found inside, he wasn't going to like it.

"Hello," he called. "Anybody home?"

He lifted the latch and kicked the door open. Standing in the middle of the room, holding her derringer, was Sarah June. She had a wild expression. Slocum followed her aim to the bed. Sanders had been stripped down, then securely tied.

"John, this bitch is crazy! Help me!"

"Shut up, Sanders," Slocum said coldly. His eyes were on the blonde woman. Her hand shook. She still had not become a cold-blooded killer.

"Don't try to stop me, John. Don't!"

"She'll kill you, too, John. She—"

"I said shut up," Slocum shouted. To Sarah June he said in a quieter tone, "Is this worth it to you? Pulling the trigger?"

"I told you what he did to my sister."

"He can be sent back to Salt Lake City. They'll hang him for what he did."

"I can save them the trouble. Like I did with the other three."

"You killed them? Heywood and Yarrow and Carson? You crazy bitch!"

Slocum stepped closer. Sarah June cocked the derringer. It never wavered from its target now. She held it in a hand made steady by her iron determination.

"I don't care if you kill me, John. I don't! I've got to do this."

"Slocum, please," Sanders pleaded. "Stop her. Shoot her where she stands."

"You did it, Sanders. You told me you did."

"Of course I did. I was drunk. I didn't know what was going on. It was all Yarrow and Heywood's doing. Carson left 'fore the fun started."

"Fun? You call what you did to Mary Beth *fun*?"

"Mary Beth? Was that her name?"

Slocum became suddenly calm. Everything came into sharp focus. He knew what he would do in this situation. Without a word, he turned and went to the door.

"Slocum, I'm begging you. Please!"

The gunshot echoed in the small cabin. Slocum stepped outside and pulled the door shut. The gunshot had spooked his horse, and it took him a few minutes to catch it and soothe it enough to mount and ride away. He never looked back. There was too much vengeance there for him to stomach.

Watch for

**SLOCUM AND THE
SCHOOLMARM**

348th novel in the exciting SLOCUM
series from Jove

Coming in February!